A FORBIDDEN AGE GAP ROMANCE

PRIDEFUL ACHE

C. S. SILVERNE

Editing: Hannah G. Wentz at English Proper Editing Services (@englishpropereditingservices)

Cover Artwork: Valerie

Interior Formatting: Disturbed Valkyrie Designs (@disturbedvalkyriedesigns)

To all the brats who back talk just a little too much sometimes. We really are just masochists who need a firm hand every now and then, huh?

ARE YOU A
LITTLE DEVIL?
CONTENT WARNINGS

The following will contain:
anxiety, barebacking, begging, bratting, breath play, death of a parent, degradation, domination, fingering, gun violence, humiliation, impact play, oral, pet play, praise, punishment, rough sex, sadism, spanking, and substance use.

Prideful Ache is a standalone novella featuring a bratty heroine, a hero that is 20 years older than her, and BDSM themes within a motorcycle club setting.

However, it is 80% smut and 20% plot. If you have expectations for a long, love-filled story… you won't find it here. You have been warned.

Character Name Pronounciation:
Aureo: (eh-row)
Phoebe: (fee-bee)

PLAYLIST

Stuck in my Head - Sleep Theory
Aqua Regia - Sleep Token
Drown - Martin Garrix (ft. Clinton Kane)
If You Only Knew - Shinedown
Stars - Skillet
Touch - MAALA
Zombie - Bad Wolves
Take Me to Church - Tommy Vext
Barely Breathing - From Ashes to New (ft. Against the Current)
In Between - Beartooth
Do I Wanna Know? - Arctic Monkeys

"To have someone give you control of their bodies and minds, to be entrusted with the responsibility to take care of them, to have someone willing to suffer for you, to forsake pride and dignity to please you... what other gift in this world can possibly equate to that? And more importantly, what makes you worthy to receive it?"

UNKNOWN

ONE

PHOEBE

There was always something so intoxicating about pain.

The impact of being slapped. The burning sting from digging my fingernails into my skin, watching how the skin only grew red and aggravated. Even the nick from a razor or snap from a rubber band, once I made it past the initial wince or groan, made my breath grow heavy.

It was euphoric, in its own sense.

Addiction was never something I struggled with,

thankfully, until the aspect of pain came into the equation. I was addicted to feeling some form of pain, but it was harder to come by than most people assumed—unless you just wanted to bang your knee into a door and then moan like a lunatic in front of a crowded room.

Yummy. Probably not recommended by a clinical physiatrist.

Or, well...anyone.

In the minds of many, the prospect of seeking pain often meant you were mentally ill or disturbed. Basically, you had to be depressed or insane, which I was neither. At least, I didn't think I was, anyway. I'm sure I've had a few boyfriends who thought otherwise, though.

The point was—I didn't seek out pain. I simply... relished in it.

Thinking someone was psychotic for liking the discomforting things in life was complete, utter bullshit, and frankly, no one's business. Everyone's a freak in their own way. Some people went as far as to have sex with rotting corpses, so in comparison, I'm a fucking saint.

Even if the occasional graveyard sex never hurt anybody.

Mostly.

That was a story for another day, though.

Aches zipped through my forearm and a sigh fell out of my mouth. Leaning back in the leather chair, I crossed my ankles, watching as my destroyed, midnight jeans grew tight against my thighs from the movement. I relished in the digging, *stinging* sensation.

It hurt.

And yet, a component in my brain nearly purred from the discomfort.

The sound of ripped disposable wax paper spread throughout the small, cramped setup of Kane's workspace and I cringed inwardly. These studded boots were great for the entire badass-biker-chick look that came with the ambiance of The Devils MC, but they were *not* practical while sitting in a tattoo chair, covered in wrap that squeaked every time my ass moved slightly to the right.

"Sorry," I muttered. Kane only grunted back in response.

He was always grunting. I was surprised he didn't speak caveman.

Fortunately, the pain of a tattoo gun was about as socially-acceptable as I could get without my father having some kind of stroke. If anyone around me thought I was at risk from an outside force—even if that force was my own brain—my MC *brothers* would form yet another biker version of a Sister Mary church circle around me.

Just like they did when fifteen-year-old Phoebe told her father that she had begun dating some boy.

It was nothing more than a Phoebe-cock-blocking-circle, but I wasn't going to say that out loud. Not the type of circle jerk people actually want to be in. Especially when Aureo, one of the new riders at the time, caught me losing my virginity in the backseat of a college guy's pickup truck, mid fake orgasm. Tits out and all.

To be fair, the random guy promptly shoved me off of him after making eye contact with Aureo—girls knew how to get themselves off in seconds, but as soon as you threw a stumbling guy into the picture, it was game-over.

Not the best way to lose your v-card, that's for sure. No one in the gang looked me in the eyes for months after that, but I didn't think it had anything to do with purity, sex, or similar. Instead, I'm pretty positive that my father would have decapitated any of his men, loyal or not, just for looking at me during that time of my life, period.

Your wife dies, your teenage daughter starts having

sex, *and* your town fills itself with rival gangs? Hell, he probably wanted to decapitate me—and it would honestly have been stress relieving if he did. I didn't envy the man for all of the attitude I threw his way.

Or the entire biker crew, for that matter.

I could still feel Aureo tugging my ponytail in the bar one day after a particularly loud argument with Daddy dearest. I tried to look at him, only to be met with a black bandana that covered most of his face. "Bratty Phoebe out to play again?" he muttered, swiping the beer from me that I had just conveniently pouted my way into receiving from the bartender. He left without another word, departing with a dark chuckle, just like he always did.

Fucking asshole.

He saw my tits *once* and thought he had some kind of bullying claim over me.

So, it wasn't a surprise any of the other brothers avoided me like the plague after that experience. They were probably one comment away from getting stabbed in the leg as it was, let alone if they brought me up.

Aureo, new rider or not though, had it lucky.

Afterall—he was dad's childhood best friend who moved away to be with the woman of his dreams, only to crash and burn after some shitty luck with love and *killing* careers. Dad protected him unlike anyone else. Sometimes, I wondered if he'd choose him or me.

I was pretty sure he would choose me, but you never really knew. A brotherhood bond went to depths even I didn't understand sometimes.

In my defense, no one wanted to lose their virginity to a fumbling boy who masturbated more hours than he slept; let alone one who didn't even know how to put on a condom correctly. Granted, no one really wanted to lose their virginity in the back of a truck, either, but my options were limited and the opportunity presented itself.

Get it done.

Get it over with.

No societal standards over the stupid hymen.

So, if pretending I wasn't an absolute masochist was the only objective needed to avoid the wild, mostly-bearded Sister Margarets, then so be it.

They had certainly cock-blocked me enough already.

"And we're done," Kane said, his voice gruff as he squinted down at the fresh ink on my arm, inspecting it one last time. Smiling, I eagerly jumped off the tattoo bench to inspect the newest design in his studio mirror. The skin was raw, pink, and heavily abused, but the wolf staring back at me was beautiful. Intricate swirls of blue danced in the eyes of the design, while the rest of the piece remained black and white, matching the other artwork dancing over my skin.

While I had never believed myself to be a spiritual person, I always wondered what it would be like to be reincarnated as a wolf. I wondered what it would be like to be *truly* fearless, loyal, and worthy, without being born in the ranks for such a position.

To earn the right of survival instead of being guarded.

I was fortunate to be the princess of such a brotherhood, but as the saying goes: you always wonder about the things you haven't experienced or don't have, and then you envy it, anyway.

So, while I would never be a wolf and I would never have to realistically worry about surviving in this life, I could carry it with me. I could carry around a semblance of strength that said I was worthy without my father's say-so. I could use my smart mouth to portray I was something strong, even if I often questioned myself during the dark hours at night.

I watched as Kane began the steps of his aftercare process, never missing a beat in the routine, smirking in admiration at his own artwork.

It was the same method every time.

Douse paper towels in foaming soap, wipe the flesh until it was nearly raw—maybe a few more times, if he was feeling extra generous that day—and then bullshit around before covering the area with a bandage that hurt like fuck to take off in a couple days.

It was like clockwork.

A sigh of relief escaped my mouth as he started to wipe the cool material against the inflamed flesh of my forearm and my shoulders slumped forward slightly. The skin around the blackened floral design was bright, pink, and hot to the touch.

The cool glide of the cleaning solution was near orgasmic because of it.

I chuckled as I thought about how so many people thought the aftercare process was similar to wiping their arm with sandpaper, when I compared it to the feeling of being doused in cold water after escaping an inflamed house.

Yet again, masochistic tendencies.

Or maybe the general population was just full of pussies.

The lines of pain, courage, and cowardice were all extremely thin and blurry in the grand scheme of things. Plus, if I could call the world overly-sensitive, then I could easily tell myself that nothing was *technically* wrong with me or my...eccentric outlets.

Earlier that evening, after the wolf design had already been drawn up and we had sipped one-too-many fingers of Irish whiskey in what we called *Birthday Bitch Celebration*, Kane and I impulsively decided to add vine work and sunflowers to the already existing Stormed Souls symbol further down my arm. I looked down in admiration with him as it blended into the rest of my artwork beautifully. I was desperate to add any feminine touch to the amount of testosterone that surrounded me, and like always, Kane delivered exactly what I needed.

Plus, I knew when I decided on the addition that my dad, president of the Little Devils MC, wouldn't have any issues with it like he would with any of the other guys who decided to mark themselves with the symbol.

I was a daddy's girl, through and through, after all.

Looking down in fondness, the florals and smoky design surrounding the infamous skull, holding a lightning bolt under its eye, glared back up at me. I couldn't contain my smile.

Dad would never let me in the field with the rest of them, but I would always be a member, anyway.

I was proud of what he accomplished.

Even if it wasn't inherently legal all of the time.

It was pretty much initiation to be tattooed by Kane at least once if you lived in the small town of Nixie, Ohio. He was the best in the area. From the minute I turned eighteen—the only law my dad was ever truly strict on, *go figure*—to now, on my twenty-second birthday, Kane had completed nine projects along my skin; with many more to come.

"I love it," I whispered, the smile on my face growing even more.

The double bright side about tattoos belonging to the *one* category of *acceptable* pain?

Art.

There would always be an artistic conclusion to the agony.

I leaned forward, placing way too much trust in the arm rail of the tattoo chair, and plopped a wet kiss on Kane's cheek, leaving the softest imprint of purple lipstick in its wake. He made a noncommittal sound, wiping away at his stark-black beard with the back of his hand as the faintest glimmer of pink formed under the scratchy skin.

"Girly, can you stop kissing me after every tattoo session? I have a lady, you know."

"Nope," I replied, popping the p with my lips. "I have to show my appreciation somehow. And your one-night stands don't count as having a lady, K. But nice try."

He laughed gruffly, the bloodshot in his eyes simmering against his blue irises, and clutched his heart mockingly. "Some guys would prefer to have a container of whiskey or a blow job for thanks, yet I get gifted with wet kisses and insults."

"Go ask your *lady* for a blow job then, old man."

He rolled his eyes and snapped the gloves off of his hands, tossing them in the waste bin by his swivel chair. "Yeah, yeah. Whatever, you brat."

I watched him, curious as to what the man was ever really thinking about. If there was ever someone to be confused by, it was Kane Rogers. He always tried to fit in with the rest of the guys, but it never really clicked. He was quiet, calculating, and yet none of us knew anything real about him, other than his artistic skills.

He was...*different*. And I never knew if that was good or not.

He avoided the topic, easily sidestepping the conversation as he pulled a bandage barrier from his drawer of supplies along with a pair of neon-pink scissors. "So, tell me. What is the famous *biker-princess* doing for her birthday?" A twisted, faux smile filled his face.

"Do you want the truthful answer or the bullshit answer?"

"What do I look like, your father? I couldn't care less, but the truth would be nice, yeah."

I bit my bottom lip. The slightest bits of nervousness fitted through my stomach with the truthful answer. "I'm going to get shit-faced."

He snorted. "Obviously."

"And then I'm going to the Crow Cavern with Echo."

His sudden stiff posture was enough to make my stomach clench.

I always attempted to not appear as shy and reserved as I actually was, but damn, telling one of your brothers that you were practically going to a sex club wasn't exactly a *pleasure*.

He looked down at me with something akin to humor in his eyes. Though as the light from his floor lamp hit his face, a scowl etched across his stern features, highlighting the rugged and scarred appearance even more. "The Crow Cavern? Ain't you a little too young for that kind of thing?"

"I thought you said you weren't my parent?" I rebutted. I felt my eyebrow twitch in annoyance.

He pointed at me, his own bushy eyebrow raising in mock defense. "I'm not. But you know that we protect you, and you and your little friend are about to walk into a sex club. Can you blame me for not loving the idea?"

"Maybe. But it is technically my dad's club, you know. I have my big girl pants on and everything lately. I know exactly what goes on in there."

"You know, one of the guys is patrolling tonight. Maybe you and Echo should ju–"

I snapped forward, cutting his sentence short, forcing the chair beneath me to creak obnoxiously. I did *not* need someone trying to be a second father to me. Especially when my real father was suffocating, albeit lovingly, enough. "I can handle myself. I don't need a bodyguard."

That bushy brow of his lowered, furrowing instead. He stared at me, his eyes calculating me yet again. But after a few moments, he raised his hands in submission, like his own personal white flag. The tattooed rose on the back of his hand glinted in the light from the action.

"Alright. Your funeral, girly. Give me your wrist so I can put this shit on and get you out of my shop. I have plans tonight."

I heaved out a breath of relief and slumped back into his chair, holding my arm up and ready so he could begin wrapping it with the Saniderm I loved more than anything. It hurt like a bitch to take off, regardless of how big the tattoo was, but I was just a little too fucked in the head to care.

As he placed it on my arm, completely ignoring my pouts, my mind wandered to the chaos that may ensue tonight. I sighed as my heart started to beat faster.

Echo was a really bad influence.

TWO

AUREO

I was surrounded by beautiful men and women. Nearly everyone was dressed in some variation of biker leather—all the way from the patrons, to the strippers—dancing their way onto men's laps. If I were any other kind of guy, I would've probably been palming my dick right in front of everyone like every other male in here.

Instead, I really wanted a fucking nap. I was fucking exhausted.

It was pitiful, honestly. I never would have believed

myself to be more bored from the sight of naked men and women, and yet here I was, practically *dying*. While I loved working with the fellow men in the beloved Stormed Souls, escaping a shitty marriage and moving here to rekindle with the man who had once saved my life—I think I much preferred riding than babysitting.

I learned that lesson very early when I had to babysit the beautiful, albeit bratty and shy, Phoebe Evans. Only to catch her over the lap of an older man who knew *nothing* about how to properly make a woman tremble.

My dick twitched at the memory of her riding him —tits out of her lacy bralette, skirt thrown up for easy access. Her head was thrown back like she was in pleasure, and yet when she met my smirking face through the window, I knew it was an act right from the start.

Her pretty face could not have been more bored from the actions of that *kid*.

But the panic that grew in them when she realized I was watching her?

Bliss.

Even more so when she began to ride him harder, her pouty lips dropping into a *real* moan when I palmed myself as I watched the sho—*Fuck*.

No.

I had masturbated enough to the famous biker princess who pretended I didn't exist, especially after that day. It was fucked up on so many levels, from her younger age to her being my best friend's daughter—the best friend I practically owed my life to.

I had learned to quell all the urges regarding Ryker's daughter. So the last thing I wanted was to get rock solid in this bar, of all places, and have one of Ryker's girls grind against it.

A man only had so much control.

It would either end in a girl getting railed while I pictured Phoebe in her place, or a girl bruising her tailbone as I shoved her off of my lap for good.

I rolled my eyes and cringed at my thoughts. Most men in this club, fuck—in this town alone—knew the two W's: whiskey and whores. Yet, here I sat, thinking about how badly I wanted to bury my cock into a girl who hated my very existence.

Don't get me wrong; I *was* like other guys. I would've loved to get my dick wet with one of the pretty girls here. It would've been so easy to charm them into my bed and fuck them until the sun came up, until we collapsed in a heap of exhaustion, only to kick them out without another glance.

I just *couldn't*. Not when Phoebe fucking Evans and the daydreams of her pretty lips around my dick entered my head. When the thoughts of her curves haunted my every wank. It felt like cheating, even though I've never had her in the first place.

Simply put, I was obsessed.

And I hated it.

Admittedly, I had stared appreciatively at quite a few corsets and other strappy tops tonight—I did have eyes, after all—but my dick continued to act like a sullen weeping willow or some shit. So, if I had it my way, I would have been getting shitfaced in my own apartment, where I could've eaten as many corn dogs as I wanted, and then rubbed one out on my own accord with raunchy, likely morally unacceptable, porn. The kind that porn that websites told me I was going to hell for searching up "illegal" activities.

It was the typical male's dream.

But no. Instead, I had to park my ass on a fancy, red, leather couch, that had probably seen more semen than a fertility clinic, and watch other horny heathens in Crows Cavern nearly molest each other. And I swore to whatever God ruled over me—if someone started having sex right next to me, I would lose my ever-loving mind.

It was illegal for strippers to fuck the patrons, sure, but it wasn't illegal for two consensual parties to fuck however they wanted to fuck, even if under the employment of the meanest bastard in the state. Plus, they didn't get paid for the fucking. Just for the near-orgasmic dances.

Everything always had a loophole.

I rested my cold beer against my head, forgoing all hard liquor in the stupor of restless anxiety crawling its way through my inside like a horde of ants, and breathed in deeply.

Just a few more hours.

"Yo!" I heard shouted from my left, making my head turn softly in the direction of Eros. I winced slightly, both from the dull ache building through my skull and the sight of him sporting a black eye. It was practically swollen shut. "What's up, man? What's a guy like you doing in a place like this? Aren't you supposed to be broodin' at your own reflection until it turns into a puddle or somethin'? You and that creepy fuckin' skull mask."

I huffed air out of my nose and crossed my arms petulantly. Even if the skull mask I wore on the bottom half of my face was starting to drive me crazy. "Ryker asks, you go. You know that. Plus, these masks are actually starting to grow on me."

"Ah, that I do. Hate the fuckin' masks, though. Ryker making us wear them on duty will forever piss me off. Bastard." He strolled up to me, dressed in a combination of blue jeans and a black button-up, almost similar to my own outfit if it weren't for my jeans being black and sporting rips at the knees. He paused for a short second and stared at me as the neon lights nearly danced over the growing, wild beard on his face. I watched as he blinked, twisting his mouth to the side in contemplation, only to promptly slump his ass directly next to mine.

Ah, to be part of a biker gang. If you're not drinking, fucking, or riding, then you're in someone else's personal space.

Joy.

He continued. "Any of these fine women catching your eye?"

A smirk crawled up my lips. "What makes you think I'm staring at the girls?"

"Okay." He paused, squinting at me for only a second before continuing. "Any of these fine, uh, *humans* catching your eye, then?"

"You never know, they could be vampires."

He blinked owlishly at me and it was really hard to smother my laugh at that point. He looked almost as defeated as a child who just lost the quarter they were going to use for their favorite gumball machine. "I strongly dislike you sometimes."

I huffed. "No, *Gretchen Wieners*, I am not finding

anything eye-baiting, eye-catching, or eye-winning tonight. I am just a lonely man with a lonely beer. Do you feel better?"

"Yes, I do," Eros grumbled, sipping a finger of scotch.

Where he obtained it in the few moments we sat down, I have no idea. Fucking wizard.

"What about that one?" he asked, nodding his head in the direction of the dance floor after a few moments. I narrowed my eyes at him, utterly confused by the now evil smile that started to grow on his face. If I were just slightly dumber, or drunker, I would've said that he looked thrilled. For a man with a black eye and an extremely disheveled beard, it was quite a sight.

I turned in the direction of the dance floor, annoyance zapping my spine like a lightning rod. "I told you, man. Not ton—"

Turns out, he was only being a complete and utter dick, playing on my wildest fantasies.

My heart nearly stopped of its own accord, only to start back up with the beat of a thousand horse hooves in battle—or maybe even the sound of thirty-plus bikers, all riding together, zipping through the lines of our small town, with music loud and laughs louder.

She was dressed like most of the other women in this joint, with dark eyeshadow the color of midnight and her hair even darker. Dark wine color stained her lips, and fuck, if my cock didn't instantly get harder at the thought of smearing her lip gloss in all the dirty ways I could think of.

My eyes raked down the rest of her. A leather pencil skirt that barely covered her ass, let alone her thick thighs, fit snug against her with a tucked top that matched her lips. Like everyone else, she decided to mix the combination of leather and lace, dark red against her creamy, ink-stained skin.

The combination made her akin to a dark goddess; it was a wonder that I didn't start drooling.

I knew those tattoos. All eight of them.

How cliche. Of all the nights I complained about my dick having the same attitude of Betty White attending a baptism ceremony, the girl who had haunted my every thought for the last six years decided to make an appearance tonight.

And at a shake joint, no-less.

The realization of that itself sprung my dick to life, right there.

I looked sideways at Eros, brow furrowing as I shot him the darkest glare I could muster. He choked on his laughter and scotch as I whispered a quick, "Fuck you," and turned back to my girl.

My girl, I thought, humorously. *Who doesn't even know I'm in love with her.*

She's beautiful enough to swallow the confidence of everyone in the room, enough that both devil and angel rested on her shoulder with delight. And yet, a blush always marred her pale cheeks when anyone commented on it.

I couldn't tell if that made her more beautiful or more frustrating.

I paused, squinting, trying to make sense of the plastic that covered her right arm as she swung her body to the beat of Bad Wolve's *Zombie.* Her feet, covered in the infamous studded boots we always heard click against the pavement when she was approaching, viciously stomped along with the beat of the drummer.

Because who didn't want to stomp their feet to a song of military woe?

The club needed a new DJ.

It was only when she lifted her arms in the air, swinging them around her friend in a drunken stupor, that I finally realized what I was looking at. *Make that nine.*

I had another tattoo to memorize.

And I was going to add that to the top of my to-do list.

"And so," Eros began again, "the princess taints herself in this story."

"This *story*?" I asked dubiously, never taking my eyes off her swaying form. I placed my beer down on the ground, knowing full well someone would likely steal or break it, but I couldn't find it in me to care. I couldn't look away from her, let alone pay attention to anything in my hands.

Until it hit me full force.

What the fuck *is she doing here?*

"You know, the fairytale story everyone always talks about—shimmering gowns, kisses under the stars with Prince Charming, and whatever else modern romance whores fantasize about."

A flush of annoyance jerked at me again.

No one would be kissing my princess, even if she was a rebellious little thing.

Not after I claimed her as mine for once and all.

I shook my head, resting my knuckles against my lips, and rasped, "That is the gayest shit I have ever heard. And you don't know anything about modern fairytales."

"First of all, even if I were in the homo of sexuals, it ain't a bad thing. Stop using it like a negative connotation, fucker. Secondly, what, oh dear one, do you believe is a modern fairytale? All we know is tits, bits, and wits."

I side-eyed him at the initial correction. I mean, he was right, but it was very odd for such a large and brutal man to care about the connotation of words. As the one who actually did have a dick or five in my mouth at some points in my life, the correction felt weird against my brain. I secretly wondered if he had, too, but I supposed it was none of my business.

But on his point, I truthfully didn't know the meaning of the modern fairytale. But the one thing I *did* know was how interesting my own fantasies were, yet how easily I managed to subdue them for the sake of other people's wishes.

I was a respectful man. I didn't spit on a girl's face or bruise her ass...unless she asked.

It didn't mean I didn't think about it, though.

It didn't mean that I wanted something...more.

And fuck, I thought about ruining my little princess more than I would ever admit.

"No," I whispered as Phoebe's back grew tense, her entire body following. Her head cocked to the side as her feet stopped their insistent stomping.

She knew I was watching.

"But I do know that there is no such thing as Prince Charmings anymore. Not in this world."

Eros whistled slowly, the sound low in his throat as he watched the girl who owned my sinful thoughts. My heart sped up even more with lottery winning luck that I didn't have a heart attack, only to nearly give out entirely when her hazy, drunken green eyes met my own. Lights danced across her skin with hues of varied purple from the overhead lights, nearly swallowing her form.

My tongue dipped out to my bottom lip as I raked my gaze down the front of my little devil, down to the swollen peak of her tits, all the way to her narrow waistline, but wide hips, and finally to her thighs before slowly raising them again.

If a gothic Barbie existed, then she would've fit the bill perfectly.

"So, if there aren't Prince Charmings, then what do princesses think about?" Eros whispered darkly, appreciating the gaze of sin incarnate in front of us.

I was going to give him another black eye if he didn't fucking stop.

I tried to think of a response quick enough, but all coherent thoughts left me as Phoebe began striding toward me, a look of annoyance on her face.

Truth be told, I didn't know.

But God, I hoped I found out. And I hoped, especially as my cock continued to brush behind my zipper for the first time that night—with her presence in front of me rather than in my own head as I fisted myself—that the beast inside my mind would finally get to play. Would finally get to *claim*.

I was tired of watching her from the shadows like she wasn't already mine.

Consequences be damned.

THREE

PHOEBE

Before my mother left us—my father, me, and the entire gang who called her family—she had braided my hair with trembling fingers and told me stories of how she and my father met.

She had said that she was a good girl and never expected to marry someone who was so much darker than her. In her exact words, with a smoky laugh as her fingers combed through my wet strands, she told me, "You know, my parents always wanted me to marry someone in a suit and I ended up with leather. But I wouldn't take it back for a second. Look what it gave me, bug."

When I had asked her why she was telling me this, she said, "Because I'm not going to be here for much longer, baby girl. You know that. But I want you to know that no matter who you fall in love with, I'm sure I'd like 'em. Just make sure to give them hell for me, yeah?"

I had crawled into her bed, just fourteen-years-old, and cried into her hair.

I didn't want my momma to go.

But life never listened to words like that.

She died just a under a year later.

The most admirable thing I found about my mother was that she refused to rot away in a hospital bed, even as her cancer was diagnosed at stage four. The doctors said it wasn't really worth the fight. It had progressed so much, the form of cancer so aggressive, that there was nothing that they could do. Or rather, the trauma of the treatment would be too aggressive. My momma didn't want to spend the rest of her days suffering when the result wasn't even guaranteed.

Why treat a sick woman when, even if it all worked, she wouldn't live but a few months longer, anyway?

I couldn't blame her for it at all.

So, she sat on the porch with my dad and her family every night, until the nights ran out.

And every day since then, I made sure to live up to her promise.

Give them hell for me.

Aureo watched me from his position on the infamous leather couch in the darkest corner of the cavern, the spot where nearly all light, even time, seemed to cease from the seclusion. If it weren't for the three spotlights surrounding the couch—spotlights we only installed just recently—then it would be nearly impossible to see him.

He was a man of the dark. And he was watching me.

Hypocritical as fuck, considering he was once again wearing a mask. He would always watch the world around him, but yet, would never let anyone watch him back.

I fucking hated when men watched me like I was something to eat. It enraged me.

And yet, heat blossomed throughout my abdomen and chest from knowing that I captured Aureo's attention. Like I was the only woman on the dance floor.

That enraged me, too. There was no reason I should feel this way towards him. I hadn't spoken to him in years, besides the occasional eye-glance or awkward mutter when we ended up at the same bar. I could have sworn that he hated my very existence. But fuck, the feeling of being watched by him made me freeze like a deer in headlights, experience the crash and burn, only to revive itself after being hit by a bolt of lightning.

And that scared me—terrified me—because that deer would have to be an act of God or evil to survive something so intense, and I didn't know if I was capable of that.

I didn't know if anyone was capable of that.

It had to be the alcohol through my bloodstream.

"Just go." Echo laughed in my ear. I hadn't even realized that I stopped dancing, or even that she had stopped dancing, too. People were starting to give us agitated looks for just standing stock-still and taking up space on the concrete floor for no good reason. Someone was bound to throw their drink at my head if I stayed there.

I just kept staring at the man who both frustrated and captivated me more than any other.

I looked at her. "What?"

"Oh, don't try to bullshit a bullshitter. A fine piece of eye candy is looking at you like he's in love with you. Plus, I know that look in your eye. Go hop on that!"

"The look of loathing and confusion in my eyes?

Really? That's what is making you say, *'go hop on that'*?"

She hummed quizzically, a small smile playing on her full mouth. Her dark complexion nearly glowed and her hair was the definition of a kinky, sex-head mess. "You're cute when you lie and deflect, ya know. If only I was feeling fruity tonight." Her hand hit my ass in a smack. "Go!"

"God, you're fuckin' crazy sometimes," I responded, shrugging her hand off my ass. I didn't know what she was getting at, given we had never experimented together in the slightest, but her comments and philosophical comments regarding my face were not my form of a fun evening. Regardless of us being raised together, going as far to even taking baths together as children, she confused the fuck out of me.

Especially when a man who really *was* eye candy was watching me.

I had enough thoughts in my brain without his presence.

Echo sighed dramatically before shooing me with her hands. "Go!"

"C'mon," I grumbled. I probably could have stomped my foot like a child. "There is no reason for me to talk to him. Aren't we supposed to have a girls' night?"

She laughed. "Yeah, babe, because a girls' night was gonna happen, anyway. Threesome? You don't even like girls, silly." She shoved at my shoulder, tipping back her chin and giving me a look that could rattle any stubborn stars. She was a scary drunk.

Grumbling under my breath, I swung my head back in the direction of Aureo, only to find his gaze still trained on me. Irritation ticked at the back of my skull again and I swore I could feel the pressure in my neck. I was going to wake up with a kink.

Why couldn't I just be gay? Men sucked.

I grunted, swallowing my pride, and began stomping to the other side of the cavern.

Now I really did *look like a child.*

I was supposed to have a one-night stand for my birthday. Not an argument.

In mere moments, I was standing in front of Aureo. I looked to his right, nodding my head at Eros —one of the weekend warriors I knew to be an absolute teddy bear—and prayed to all the heavens that he would take the hint.

Thank God, he did.

"I'll take that as my cue," he said, chuckling. He turned his head back to mine and it took all my power to not scowl back at him as he winked. Before he passed me, he leaned down slightly, his whiskey breath hitting my ear. "Get 'em, princess."

He walked away and my eyes trailed after him in exasperation.

Why did everyone in this damn place want me to ride Aureo like a mechanical bull?

I turned my head back to Aureo, ready to blow a short-fuse, but stopped when I saw the look on his face. He was still watching me, although I couldn't see anything below the mask that covered the second half of his face. It was *unnerving*. The brown in his eyes nearly danced at me, humor and something akin to warmth watching my every movement.

It made my stomach lurch.

He stayed quiet, making me speak first. "Can I help you with something?"

He snorted, but that was it.

You have got to be kidding me.

"That's it? You're just going to stalk me, eye-fuck me, and then turn into a broody alpha-male who grunts like a caveman?"

Nothing. Absolutely nothing, except for the slightest twitch in his brow.

"You could at least tell me what you want. It would be the gentleman thing to do," I said as my hands went up to my hips nervously. My shirt had ridden up to the point that my belly-button piercing was showing, skin slick with sweat, but I couldn't find it in me to truly care. I was confident with my body, and if he was staring at me anyway, then what did it matter to be modest?

My jaw, however, went slack as he leaned forward, picked up a beer on the floor right next to his leather boots, nearly covered by his black jeans, lifted his mask just enough for me to see the square cut line of his jaw and pairing stubble, and took a deep swallow. All while keeping eye contact with me.

What a *dick*.

"Right. Because I expected a merc like you to know human dialect, anyway."

If a human akin to the devil could have turned into a statue, he would have, right before my eyes. Yet, he still said nothing. Now, it was just a staring contest with an evil incarnation. My body nearly vibrated from the brewing anxiety and loud, thumping music surrounding us.

You are an independent woman. You don't deserve this, I screamed inside my head.

I scoffed. Echo must have been delusional by thinking that Aureo had any interest in me. But, I couldn't blame her, even if I could have gotten better responses from a brick wall than *him*.

"Why did I bother coming over here?" I muttered as I began to turn away from him. I was right. I was an independent woman. I wasn't a child anymore. Yet, I couldn't help but feel the slightest bit of dejection as I turned away from him. I wasn't the type of girl who needed a man's approval, and I certainly wasn't the girl who needed sex daily, but it still stung in some weird way.

I barely made it a single step before I felt a tight, heated pressure on my wrist. By instinct, I scowled, looking down and making eye contact with a hand that may have well resembled a bear's paw. He had me captured in his grip, and right when I went to tug against him—now too pissed to give a damn about what he wanted—I felt the lightest brush of the plastic covering his face against my cheek, sending a shiver down my spine. Considering I hadn't known he was behind me, it's a miracle that I didn't jump out of my skin.

"What the fuck did you just say to me?" he rasped.

I turned to him, meeting his hardened gaze and tugging slightly to try and get out of his grasp. "I asked what the reason for me coming over here was, only to be ignored by the brute barbarian you apparently are."

My words only made him hold on to me tighter, but I kept my expression sharp. "Are we done now?"

His jaw clicked, only slowly releasing when he took in a shuddering breath, cracking his neck to the side.

Finally—an *emotion*. Good for him.

"Not that," he muttered. His voice sounded like he had just swallowed the smoothest whiskey and goosebumps broke out against my skin. "And quit with the pompous, bitch act. It's annoying."

You have got to be kidding me.

I said as much. "Are you fucking kidd—"

He cut me off, squeezing my wrist tighter. "What did you call me a minute ago?"

Anger seared through me. Now he *was really* acting like a brute barbarian. I was going to wake up with bruise marks on my wrist, of all places, tomorrow morning. I felt my teeth ground together from the realization.

When I admitted my love of pain to the class, this was *not* what I meant.

He pulled my wrist back behind my back, twisting my elbow until I grunted softly. One of his rough, calloused hands moved to my front until he was holding my throat in a solid grasp. I felt his chuckle, the breath hot, as he felt me gulp against him.

I would have never admitted this to anyone, but

being held like that made the most depraved thoughts enter my head. I could feel my heart beating faster, maybe even begin beating elsewhere, and I swore he could feel it too as my thighs squeezed together on their own doing.

"What did you call me?" he whispered into my ear, repeating himself and squeezing the hand on my throat softly.

I gulped. I was still so fucking pissed—seething, probably vibrating, actually—but being a girl in this world meant you knew your limits, and my limits stopped at being withheld by the big, bad wolf.

"People are going to notice you holding me like this," I whispered, forgoing any attempts to try and pull away from him. I had a feeling that whatever was happening, whatever had fallen over the both of us, I wasn't going to win. And I was right. He pulled me closer to him until my back was flush against the soft material of his shirt.

We almost fit together like puzzle pieces.

I rolled my eyes at the thought. This was *not* the time to be poetic.

"See if I give a flying fuck, little girl. I'm not going to ask again."

My subconscious thought back through the last few minutes. It was hard to think around him as he touched me, especially as the unique scent of his cedarwood, nearly geranium cologne hit my senses. It was almost intoxicating in its own right.

I was pissed not even five minutes ago, yet now I fought the urge to melt into him. The power of alphamales was seriously something that needed scientific research.

Finally, expletives floated through my brain as I realized what Aureo was really asking for. My body went taunt against him and I cursed under my breath when his grip tightened even more, almost to the point that breathing was difficult.

He knew that I knew.

"I called you a merc," I said, all of my bravado fading with fear and the most confusing sense of hot arousal in its tracks. His touch was searing, the calluses on his hands scraping against my flesh. I wanted it off me, but yet I wanted it to consume me at the same damn time.

Years ago, when I was still a young, dumb teenager, I overheard my father talking about Aureo in his study. It was merely days after Aureo had caught me losing my virginity and I was searching for any speck of dirt I could use against the new rider, regardless of the powershift between us.

He had told my father about me being with a boy. *What else could I have done?*

During that act of spying, me creeping up to the door and nearly putting my ear against the hard, oak wood, I heard my father call Aureo "odder than others," and "akin to a goddamn mercenary." I had tucked it away in my brain as a *just in case* knowledge box.

I had also tucked my tail in between my legs when my dad opened up the door and a tattooed arm jumped out to catch me right when I fell from the sudden disappearance of the wood. A look akin to horrified confusion covered his face. I had lied and told him I was about to knock on the door to ask what he wanted for dinner. While I didn't know if he bought it, neither of us ever brought up the topic again.

Until now.

Except, no Daddy dearest was in sight to save me now.

Aureo exhaled heavily behind me. The breath forced even more goosebumps to spread over my body, now covering the skin from the base of my neck to the insides of my wrists, and I knew he felt everything. "That's right. Now, tell me why you called me that, little girl."

I looked up into the bar, watching the strippers dance, and I heavily wished that I hadn't walked over here. I would have rather walked into an orgy down the hall than have dealt with that conversation. I kept my voice resilient, though. He may know the effect he had on my body, but I would be damned if he knew the inside of my brain.

"Because you are, aren't you? I heard my father call you one, years ago. An ex-con. A criminal. A mercenary." I spit the last part out, unbothered by how angry my voice seemed, even when I was anything but.

Truthfully, I couldn't care less if he was an ex-criminal. That would almost make me a hypocrite, considering the people I called my friends and family. I just needed to act the part now and having an attitude was the only way I knew how to do that.

Silence met me for a beat. "No, little devil. I am not a fucking *mercenary*."

I blinked. "You're not?"

"No, I'm not. Nor am I an ex-con. *Yet*."

Oh shit.

"Yet?" I breathed out. I swore my heart began galloping to the sound of hooves in war.

That *stupid,* dry laugh sounded yet again as alarm bells blared through my head. I was down for a lot of kinky, disturbing things, but I drew a line at homicide.

He purred, and I swore I felt his tongue brush the

underside of my ear. "I might be by the end of the night. Now, I think you need to get on your knees and apologize. You pissed me off and I'm tired of you wearing my patience down to nothing."

That indignation I knew so well moments ago hit me again. Who the hell was he to ask me to get on my knees in a public bar? In *my dad's* bar?

"Excuse me? Who do you think you are? I am not your puppet."

"Oh, I beg to differ, little one. Now, I am getting extremely tired of repeating myself, but I will one last time. Get on your *fucking* knees."

Adrenaline traveled throughout my entire nervous system like cocaine traveled through the bloodstream. Between his grip on my throat, his voice against my ear, and the lethality of his words—I was finding it extremely hard to breathe.

I *was* an independent woman, strong and fierce, but I also knew there was nothing wrong with being submissive for the right man. And yet, I still wanted to push his buttons. He expected a form of obedience from me when he hardly *knew* me. I wanted to make his skin crawl in the heated way he forced mine to do, and I wanted it to be painful.

I nailed the last head of my coffin.

Or maybe...what I did was exactly what he wanted instead.

"Make me," I rasped, watching as the clock ticked on the other side of the bar. It looked emptier now than it had just moments ago and I had no clue as to why. People normally didn't begin leaving until three, sometimes four in the morning. "You won't. You said it yourself. You've kept a distance from me, apparently. You won't make me do anything."

Aureo released his grip on my wrist and I moaned softly from the release in pressure. I twisted it back and forth, trying to ease any of the discomfort, but froze again when his now-free hand moved to the base of my hair and gripped it tight, tugging until my head was at a sharp angle on his shoulder. I whimpered loudly as he spoke. "Are you sure you want me to do that, sweetheart? That could be a mistake. After all, I don't normally fuck childish *brats*."

I seethed, trying to pull away from his grip. He could make me out to be some innocent child all he wanted, but I knew myself better than anyone did. I knew exactly how my thighs trembled when I touched myself. I knew exactly how much pain I could take until I was screaming in euphoria. And I knew exactly how to disassemble a man like him until he was nothing.

"Are you sure about that? It sure looks like you're wanting to fuck one," I spit, though smirked as I ran a palm over the bulge in his jeans. He flinched at my touch, his hand going to rub his jaw, only to hit the plastic on his face, making him growl.

He hummed against me, his chest nearly vibrating against my back. My head was still at that odd, almost painful angle, and his eyes danced in the most erotic tandem as they met mine.

I had sealed my fate then.

"I hoped that was gonna come out of that pretty mouth. Let's see how pretty that mouth can really be."

I was ready to snap at him again when he tugged me against him even more, making me take a step backwards. My back nearly bowed from the angle he kept me at.

"Turn around," he ordered. A shuddering breath escaped as I, for the first time that night, finally did something he requested. He probably would have broken my back if I kept up any stubborn trade. He kept the grab on my hair tight, though finally let go of my throat, just for a moment. I nearly choked as I took mouthfuls of air back into my lungs. He moved his free hand to cup my jaw and I frowned when his eyes softened in the slightest way. "You've been bad tonight, baby. Fuck, you've been bad the past four years. What should I do about that, huh?"

I shrugged.

Silent *piss off*'s were a specialty of mine lately.

He smirked, but only shook his head. "I think you need an attitude adjustment, little Phoebe."

"Fuck you," I spit out, trying to reel my head back. Did he truly think I was a seven-year-old girl who had forgotten to do her homework? If he wasn't going to touch me in a way that I liked, then I wasn't going to respect him.

That softness that coated his features seconds ago hardened into something akin to fury, disappointment, and buried lust, nearly making me stagger back. He stared at me a moment longer before he sat down, promptly shoving me to my knees in the process. They cracked as they hit the ground and I ground my teeth together, keeping the whimper from falling out of my mouth.

I didn't know if I wanted to gag from touching this floor, deck him for manhandling me, or weep at his feet like the horny siren in me screamed to do *from* the manhandling. Yet, everything in me seemed to freeze when he reached behind his back and pulled out a gun.

A *fucking* gun.

His finger wrapped around the trigger, just as his other hand took off the *goddamned* safety.

Fuck.

Double, triple, quadruple fuck.

Why did I have to have a mouth?

God? It's me again.

He pointed the pistol to the ceiling and my heart nearly gave out entirely when it fired. I heard a scream and the thuds of a few drunken people tripping over their own feet. I'm sure proper terror was flowing through them more than ever.

My ears were ringing, and I didn't know if it was from disbelief or fear.

Debris fell from the ceiling and I knew that if I didn't die from the man in front of me, I might if concrete started falling on my damn head.

"Get out," Aureo snarled as he kept a firm grip on my shoulder. For a short few seconds, I had completely forgotten about everyone around me. It took the sound of dozens of feet and rushed whispers for me to truly realize how we were the complete focal point of attention now.

I was going to die tomorrow, if I didn't tonight.

My father was going to auction me off. That was it.

He repeated himself again, exactly as the music in the entire bar went out. The sounds of people's footsteps sprinting out mixed with the sound of my heart-beat in a crushing rhythm.

"Out!"

Fuck me, he sounded like a mad-man. I knew I should have held onto the fear clouding my brain as tight as I possibly could.

Yet the disturbed part of my brain couldn't help but feel *hot*.

To know that I was the cause of that change in him, until his eyes looked as crazed as he sounded, made an ache develop in both my head and in between my thighs.

It had been way too long since I'd had good sex.

I heard Ero's voice behind me, as timid as a grown man's voice could be. I didn't dare take my eyes off of Aureo's to check. "Are you gonna be okay, Phoebe?"

Aureo snared. "She'll be fine. You know that."

"I asked her," Ero persisted—well, nearly growled, actually.

My head hurt. And fuck, I was getting really tired of alpha-males being growly and having pissing contests.

Why I answered the way I did, I didn't know at the time. I should have admitted myself into a mental institution, honestly.

Any sane woman would have begged Eros to drag them out of the situation I found myself in.

But the sting Aureo had already delivered me a few times so far?

I needed more of it.

I craved to see what he really wanted to do to me.

My voice shook, but I answered nonetheless. "Uh... uh, yeah. I'll be okay. I promise," I started, then hesitated. "If you find my body tomorrow, make sure my dad tears Aureo's balls off."

Ero chuckled behind me. "Will do, kid."

I heard him hesitate, likely looking at Aureo for something, though his footsteps sounded moments later.

An infinity later, the door slammed, the club was stock empty, and we were fully alone.

I gulped.

What the fuck have I gotten myself into?

FOUR

AUREO

For years, I had fantasized about the thought of this girl on her knees for me. From the moment I saw her tits through that goddamn truck window, and the way her pink tongue looked when she opened her mouth to moan—moan for me and not that fucking *kid*—I knew she would always own a piece of me. And now, while she was on her knees for me, her doe, glossy eyes looking up at me, I knew I was an absolute goner.

She was *mine*, even if she rejected it.

But even as precious as this girl was to me, she still needed punishment. And fuck if I didn't relish in the thought of punishing her until she was weeping. A part of me felt the slightest bit of guilt for hurting her, for scaring her with the pistol. The way she jumped and froze will forever be stuck in my memory. But the evil, twisted part of me purred at how she *finally* listened to me.

Her voice was timid as she spoke, her jaw working in a tandem. "Why did you make them leave?"

I leaned forward, spreading my legs slightly and urging her to shuffle closer as I cupped her jaw in one of my massive hands. My thumb stroked at her jaw and I nearly groaned at how she seemed to relax from the movement. My girl *did* have a soft side.

Regardless, I answered, "I don't share."

Her back went rigid again. I couldn't help but smile as I moved my thumb to her pouty lips. Her eyes were so green, so bright they could've matched the damn Cathedral Beaches in Spain. Of my own home. It was far too tempting. "You don't own me, Aureo."

I couldn't help the way my grip tightened on her jaw and I prayed that I didn't bruise her pretty face. I wanted to bruise a lot of parts on this girl, but not there. She was far too pretty for marks on her jaw.

But this girl was *the girl*, and it made feelings I

didn't even know I was capable of feeling anymore spread through my chest, including a raged jealousy from the thought of other men touchin' what was mine.

"I do, though. Do you want me to prove it to you?"

The question stunned her into silence and I swore her eyes grew to be even larger. My dick really started to strain against my zipper, and I would've been a lyin' man if I said it didn't hurt to draw this out as much as possible.

She needed to earn the pleasure, though.

I continued. "I know that there are a great deal of things that I want to do to you, but I won't do them if you don't want me to."

She hesitated, but I swore I saw her knees shift together slightly, almost like she was easing an ache in between her legs. And I swore a part of my soul roared from the smallest act. Her voice was timid and husky, all at once. "What do you want to do to me?"

"Oh, little girl. I want to see you bent over at all angles. I want to see you swallow my cock down that pretty little throat until you're crying, unable to breathe. I want to see your body covered in bruises and marks. I want to fill you up until you don't think you can take it anymore and then spank you until you're raw. How does that sound?"

A blush marred her cheeks, brighter than ever. "Uhm...okay..."

I chuckled as I petted her like a dog. Just a little animal in heat, too dumb to answer questions after all her barks. "Okay? Just okay? I've fantasized it, all the way until you're screaming in pleasure *and* pain. Fuck, little girl, if I had a marker, I would write *brat* across your forehead for how you've acted tonight." I hummed under my breath as I continued sweeping my thumb across her bottom lip. The light-pink lipstick that covered that pout smeared slightly, sweeping onto her chin. The sight itself could've brought me to my knees. "But you'd like that, wouldn't you? Admit it. You want this as much as I do. It's why you haven't said the word *no* once tonight."

She visibly shuddered, almost like a ghost trailed its cold fingers down her spine, and just continued to stare at me. But the war raging through those eyes told me everything I needed to know.

The biker princess of Stormed Souls was already a part of the dark side, and even if she didn't involve herself into the darkest of elements, she wanted to play with the abyss.

Finally, she spoke. "You're right."

"I'm right about wha—"

"Just for tonight," she interrupted, her tone carrying that goddamned stubborn quality.

Like hell. I would claim her in most senses tonight —make her my lady for the world to see, even if that scary motherfucker of her father tried to kill me—and she would know it.

Instead, and call me a sadistic fuck for being incapable of admitting the truth in the moment, I nodded. "Just for tonight."

FIVE

PHOEBE

"Just for tonight," he whispered.

I fit perfectly in between his spread legs. It was almost like I belonged there, staring up at him, holding his calf like a child would their parent when they were begging for something. I could feel the heat of his touch like a branding iron, his thumb constantly rubbing against my bottom lip in soothing strokes.

And it fucking *terrified* me.

No man had ever affected me like this. I didn't know how to feel about it.

Which is why I was an absolute wimp and nearly begged him to agree that this would end after the night was over, even if it felt wrong to the strongest degree. I didn't know how people were able to breathe when they were captivated with another human so much, for such a small amount of time. Especially when that human started treating you like you were a lover *and* a whore.

He was simply everything in that moment, and I was a coward.

"Are you sure?" Aureo asked once more. He never moved his brown, deep gaze away from my own. For him to be a man who belonged to the Stormed Souls, he was surprisingly very clean-cut. He could easily have fit the bill of wearing a suit in a major company just as well as he could ripped jeans and leather vests on machines of steel.

I nodded in response. I think my voice would have cracked if I said anything.

"Good," he nearly purred. "Now, rub my cock through my jeans, little one." His fingers moved away from my mouth, only to cup my jaw once more. Maybe for the second time that night, I listened to him. I truly wanted nothing more than to curse the seven heavens when I noticed how my hand was shaking.

It wasn't like I was a saint by any definition of the word.

I had sex. A lot of it.

And still, my hand shook like it was my first time giving a man a hand job. Anxiety clawed at my brain. I was terrified of the man before me, yet my pussy ached for his touch—for his tongue. He aroused me in the most commanding ways, and I couldn't tell if it was pleasure or humiliation that scoured me.

His gaze moved down from my face, following my hand, and a harsh breath escaped his clenched teeth when I palmed his length. Even behind the rough material of his jeans, he felt thick and hard, I swore I almost gulped. I felt the slightest tremor through Aureo's arm.

He continued, nearly growling. "Take it out."

I stilled, my caresses stopping entirely. "You take it out. You're the one who seems to have such good control of it. Look, it's hard and everything!" With added affect, I tapped his dick in a petting gesture. *"Good boy."*

"Take my cock out of my jeans." His voice was

harsher. I looked up at him to see his lips curling back in a snarl of sorts. "Am I going to have to repeat everything I say all fucking night?"

Finally.

I was finally able to go back to exactly who I was: that girl fought anything with a pulse. Even if it ended in me getting my ass kicked.

"I don't know. Are you going to *softly* demand things like you're entitled to them all night long? I could be hard of hearing, you know. Isn't a real man supposed to take what he wants?" I bit back, purposely squeezing his length harder than necessary, causing him to flinch just slightly.

He would be fine.

Maybe.

I honestly didn't care at that moment. *Fuck* how he was talking to me.

Our eye contact could have waged wars, though we settled for our war alone. Anger seared me. It was a battle of wills, and I would have been damned if I said it didn't excite me more.

"Move," he nearly growled—barked, actually—at me. His heated grip moved towards my hair and he pulled hard enough that tears began to line my vision.

"What?" I asked incredulously.

"I am *not* going to repeat myself again, Phoebe. You fucking heard me. God, should I just go home and jerk off to my wall at this point?"

Slowly, heart dropping the slightest bit, I shuffled back a few inches.

Humiliation and uncertainty clawed at my brain now; I could feel my face blushing to the heat of an inferno. My hand moved off of his crotch, drifting down to the skin exposed by the rips in his jeans, just as his touch left my brown locks.

I gaped at him as a feeling similar to rejection flitted through me next.

Sure, I was being a bitch, but I didn't expect him to completely deny me.

Regardless of our battle of wills, he was as intoxicating as the whiskey streaming through my blood.

I didn't want it to end so soon.

He leaned forward with me and my face scrunched up as he started to remove the black belt secured around his waistband. It slid through loop after loop, the sound methodic, and I flinched when he snapped it out entirely, inches from my face. My gaze moved back to his face and I froze again.

He fucking *smiled* at my flinch.

"What's your favorite safe word, pretty girl?"

I blinked. "What? What is that?"

"You've been having sex with these men and they never taught you about safe words?"

"No..." I led, a blush forming.

"*Jesus fuck*. You're done fucking all these little boys. Your safe word with me is *lavender*, do you understand?"

Hope bloomed in my chest, for some ungodly reason. He wasn't ending the night. "Yes, sir."

"Good. You'll only use it when you can't take something I do to you. Do you understand? Whenever you say it, I'll stop. And I'm a man, sweet girl. I'll stop for the night and we won't continue at all."

I felt like I was in a fever dream.

He continued, snapping the belt in front of my face so I jumped and looked back at him. "Repeat it for me, baby."

"Lavender."

"Oh look, she does do what she's told sometimes. *Good girl.*"

Fuck. I was going to combust on the spot.

Why was being talked down to so *fucking* hot?

I only had a moment to recoup, the urge to call him a dick on the tip of my tongue—to keep my bravado—before he lurched forward and looped the belt around my neck, cutting my gasp off entirely when he pulled it tight and secured it the buckle around my throat. Immediately, I had the urge to start coughing and I moved my hands up to grasp the buckle, trying to pull it off of me. I struggled, pulling and panicking, eyes bulging as tears sprung down my face automatically.

"Leave it," he ordered. "It'll get easier. Unless you start acting out again. Then I'll just keep pulling it tighter, and tighter, until your goddamn throat constricts on itself. You think I care about your princess status? You're the one breathing heavy for it. Maybe I should just leave you here, blue in the face, until you can act right."

Fear spread throughout my chest faster than water seeping from a broken glass. And for the first time that night—I was glad that I was on my knees.

But I listened. For some ungodly, unknown reason, I listened.

This was fucking idiotic. Aureo was nearly twice my age and he was my father's ride or die.

I thank God there weren't any cameras in this bar. I would be horrified if anyone saw me like that. Hell, I was horrified, just from the man before me.

Yet, here I sit, with a fucking belt on my throat like it's a dog collar.

Slowly, I lowered my hands down to his legs again. My throat was already restricting itself from how badly

I wanted to gasp down mouthfuls of air. But I wasn't going to push him until I was adjusted to the new sensation.

Aureo purred, "Good girl," as his hands returned to my face and hair. "Good fucking girl. Take my cock out of my zipper, little devil. Careful of the metal. I don't wear briefs, ever."

I shuffled forward again and practically groaned as my knees dug into the hard floor. I would need a pillow if I was going to spend the entire night down there, on the floor, like his goddamned *puppy*.

Nevertheless, I did exactly as he asked of me. Without the loud crowd that typically filled Crows Cavern, or the music that was even louder, the sound of his zipper sliding down and over his length could have echoed, if it weren't for both of our harsh breaths. I maneuvered his jeans just slightly, unbuttoning the metal holding them together, before my fingers met the soft flesh of his member. Doing as he said, my breath stuttering, I shifted his dick out of his jeans, narrowly avoiding the metal.

Holy hell, he was *thick*.

Sure, I had slept around some, but even then, I wasn't certain this thing could even fit inside my mouth.

I didn't even like big dicks.

They *hurt.*

His grin only widened as he stared down at me. He moved his fingers back towards my mouth, only to shove two of his large fingers in my mouth. I wretched as I felt the pad of his index and middle finger against the back of my tongue, wholly unprepared for the movement. My head kicked back, trying to fight, but he only raised one of his brows as his other hand moved to the belt buckle, ready to tighten it again.

I was going to kill him.

Or he was going to kill me.

Or I was going to kill myself for noticing how my pussy clenched in need from the threat.

Regardless, only one of us would walk out of here tonight. I was sure of it.

He explored my mouth with his fingers, the calloused pads of his fingers so used to rubbing against the metal grooves of a bike now pressed against the inside of my cheek. I let him, refusing the urge to bite, up until he suddenly shoved his fingers down my throat once more. I lurched forward into him, the sliver of skin from my crop top meeting the leather material of the couch, gagging and coughing as my stomach lurched with me.

This was so fucking humiliating. I was going to throw up on the man who, for some unknown reason, thought finger fucking the pussy equates to the mouth as well. Tears escaped the corners of my eyes.

Aureo shushed me, his thumb wiping away the tear with a faux pout on his face. Only to take the wet fingers from my mouth, coated in my spit, and suck them clean himself, tasting the last shreds of my dignity. "That's it, little one. Drool all over my hand like the slut you were before I owned you. Ah, ah. One more time," he urged, shoving his fingers down my throat again. Just like he asked, I gagged and felt tears begin to roll down my face even more.

He couldn't be serious.

"Please," I begged around his fingers. "No more."

He chuckled darkly, but showed pity and complied with me, nonetheless. He pulled his fingers out of my mouth and I breathed a sigh of relief—as much as I could with the restriction around my throat, anyway. I watched his gaze filled with lust from the drool connecting us together. Just from those two reflex checks, I was breathless.

Faster than a blink, he started sucking on his own fingers, still coated with my spit.

Fuck, I was *aching*. I had never wanted to be filled so much before.

His steel gaze hesitated for only a moment, his fingers still in his mouth, before he moved quickly again. He took his hand out of his mouth, only to wrap his fist around his dick, covering it with both of our spit. A grunt of pleasure left him and my clit pulsed with need from the sound. But he didn't stop. He stroked himself, hard and fast, like he was going to cum all over my face in seconds.

He was so hard—the veins against the underside of his shaft bulging—and I desperately began to ache with the need of being filled as he continued to stroke himself again.

Fuck.

Double fuck.

Triple fuck.

I would let him humiliate me. I would let him write on me with a fucking Sharpie at this point. I needed him.

I begged again, nearly whimpering. *"Please, Aureo."*

He moaned as he spread his legs slightly, cocking his head and tipping his head up. If he weren't wearing a mask, I'd assume the cruelest of smirks would be on his face, even as he made more room for me. "Please, *what*? Huh? Didn't you want to be a brat and call the shots? What are you begging for then, hmm? Does that slutty mouth even have a purpose?"

"You. This. Fuck, I don't *know*."

A deep laugh left his mouth, ending in a groan as he tightened his fist around his cock. The slick sounds made my face blush a bright red. Watching him jerk off while I was sitting right here, ready to use, was humiliating in a way that I didn't know was possible. A flit of emotions went through me. Rejection, arousal, fear, but most of all—desperate aches. "Aw, poor wee lamb doesn't know what she wants," he said as he grabbed my hair in a firm grip, yanking forcefully. "From how you've acted, I should just finish on your pretty face and go home. Leave you to finish yourself off. Know that you'd see my face when you play in between your legs tonight. Chasing what I denied you of."

Outrage filled me with the threat and I yanked against his hold, fighting the whimper it wanted to create deep in my throat. He was one of *those* guys. "You wouldn't be the first, dickweed," I spit. "Do you need to hear stories of all the men who sucked? Should I add you to the roster list? Like you would even know how to make a girl come, anyway. You probably wouldn't be able to tell the clit from the asshole if you tried, *little boy*."

Suddenly, the air from my throat was restricted even more, the belt tightening in response to my crude words. His other tore at my hair and I nearly felt a vein pop in my head from the mixture. I couldn't even gasp. Air strangled in my chest, stagnant. Aureo tightened the buckle, his cock forgotten about, up until I was genuinely terrified of choking on my own lungs.

It was maddening, having so little control.

And yet my pussy ached wildly for more.

I pulled at the belt around my throat wildly, scratching my own throat with my nails in my attempt to escape, only to have both of my hands captured in one firm, bruising grip and raised above my head.

Jesus, *fuck*. My father was going to find me dead in the morning, all over needing one of his rider's cock.

Shame burned me.

Fear lit me aflame.

"The more you struggle, the more you are convincing your brain to panic. Stop, baby girl. You're fine," Aureo said, his voice softer than it had been the past hour as he urged me to be still.

Slowly, seconds burning into minutes, I convinced my body to accept the harsh change. My breaths were shallow, body trembling.

Even as I knew that I was properly *dripping*.

"That's it," he said again. "That's my good, dirty girl. I told you to behave, and you didn't. This is what happens to brats. Brats get punished. They get punished until they're raw and choking. Do you want to behave yet? This can be so much better for you if you do."

"Fuck," I panted out, "you."

Wrong answer.

He stood abruptly, towering over my kneeled frame, and I watched as his cock bobbed from the motion. His face twisted in a mix of anger and lust, and from that angle, his twelve o'clock shadow contrasted darkly against his light skin.

He looked more sinister than ever.

I had never wanted to take a picture of a man more than I did right then.

My face was directly in front of his hard length, nearly pointed at me, still wet with my drool. Conflicting emotions aside, my mouth filled with drool from the sight.

"Suck," he ordered.

My lungs still hurt from how badly I wanted air. Fuck this. I still couldn't even breathe, but he wanted me to suck his dick? I shook my head.

"I'm giving you a choice, Phoebe. Don't make me take that away from you."

I pulled his own trick against him, saying nothing. Silent treatment.

He glowered at me. I couldn't tell if the dancing in his eyes was a trick of the lights still moving around us or if he was truly another variation, sinful and daunting, of the man I had known all of these years.

Seconds passed.

"Pinch my leg twice, with all of your strength, if you can't handle this. That is your new safe action since you won't be able to talk," he murmured. He gripped me by the front of the suffocating leather, tugged me forward, forcing it to choke me once more, and shoved the first few inches of his cock into my mouth.

Ashamedly, I coughed and sputtered, drooling as I choked on his girth.

That was not how I pictured the night going and a blush settled its way over my entire torso and face. I had wanted to be better than a gagging mess.

We both inhaled a sharp breath at the new sensation, air whooshing in between his clenched teeth as his hips elevated slightly. A choked gasp left me from the feeling of his silken skin as he forcefully pushed himself deeper into my mouth, cautions long gone. My eyes watered from the intrusive feeling as it pushed against my throat, his tip hitting it once, twice, forcing a heave out of me again and again. It filled my mouth entirely, shaped in a perfect circle with lipstick gliding along his entire length. The way my brain went entirely quiet from the abrupt change in our power was astounding.

Almost as if I belonged right there.

Both of his hands moved until he was clutching my scalp, hair bunching underneath his bruising grip, as he continued to thrust into my mouth, completely and utterly fucking it.

He hardly even let me truly adjust to his size before he was thrusting into me unabashedly hard. There was no time to adjust. There was no time to even breathe.

At that moment, my only purpose was to make him feel good and he knew it.

"*Don't fuckin' bite*," Aureo shuddered, moaning, as my teeth scraped against him. I rolled my eyes at his comment.

While I had threatened to remove quite a few appendages in my youth, I would never actually bite off someone's cock.

That was way too bloody for my taste.

Eventually, my mouth was finally able to accommodate his size, though he never ceased his movements, even when drool began sliding across the both of us. We moved in a perfect union of bobbing and thrusting, moaning and gagging, thrumming with pleasure and angst.

For the smallest of moments, he kept nearly his

entire length down my throat, keeping my head at a standstill with my nose smushed against his pelvis while we both moaned and heaved, only to resume his forceful movements.

Drugging.

Being used and abused in this way was drugging.

"Goddamn, little girl. Fuck. Just like that. All the way down again," he panted, letting go of my head to squeeze my shoulders. *"Please."*

The pleasure had consumed him too much and I couldn't help but tease him.

I popped his dick out of my mouth loudly, smiling up at him as I continued to fist his slick length. He was covered in my own saliva, and while I couldn't see his torso from underneath his dark button-up, I knew his abdominals were flexed, given how tight his entire body seemed. I could have probably milked him just like that.

He looked down at me, expression hard when I stopped. "Now look who's begging. Maybe you're not as tough as you seem."

"Shut the *fuck. Up,*" he replied, his control shredding in half. His hands, rough and used, moved back to my head. He gripped tight as he led his cock back into my mouth, only to begin his ministrations at his original, abusing pace.

My eyes rolled from it.

His cock hit the back of my throat repeatedly, over and over again, and I swore that the most disturbed man could have blushed from the sounds he was inflecting on us. I gagged against his length until I was out of breath, nearly retching, but never stopping.

I would be damned if I pinched his leg twice.

It was a painful, abusing pace. And I fucking loved it.

Flattening my tongue against him, I ran it along the base of his dick, even as Aureo continued to make me gag against him. He moaned louder, indicating he was close, and the sound nearly ricocheted through my entire nervous system. Regardless of our fight for dominance, my legs pressed so tightly together that I wouldn't have been surprised if I started to grind against his legs.

I was desperate to please him, to teach him that I wasn't only good for bratty retorts, but I was also desperate to be fucked until the sun came up at this point.

And fuck, seeing him uncaged was going to be my undoing.

As if he read my thoughts, he shoved me off of him. Spit pulled from my lips to his dick. We were both breathing so heavily that it almost looked like we had run a marathon. His belt still dangled at my throat like a loose snake, and I knew my makeup had to be smeared all the way from my eyeshadow to my lipstick from his assault.

I couldn't find it in me to care. I felt high.

After a moment of staring at me, he pulled me up from the knot against my neck, nearly lifting me just from the belt itself, only to lift his mask up slightly and crush his mouth to mine. I pushed against him at first, trying to escape the feeling of his soft, yet firm mouth and plastic mask outline. His facial hair scratched against my face. He was rough, wild, and evil. If it weren't for his grip on the belt, I would have evaded him, but he was ruthless and demanding in his persuasion for attention.

I felt the brush of his tongue against my bottom lip, yet I still shoved at him. I knew that if I gave in to the kiss, I would be done for. Aureo would own a part of me forever.

After a moment of the fight, I felt Aureo tighten that *damned* belt even further against my throat. I gasped into him as he jerked the buckle into place, nearly suffocating me entirely. My hand flew up in response, knocking the mask off his face entirely, and I didn't have it in me to care.

I was going to wake up bruised and raw the next day. Over a *belt*.

He took advantage of my submission, shoving his tongue into my mouth. I couldn't help but moan into him as our tongues began to dance wildly with the other. He moved his knee in between my thighs, rubbing gently, and it was entirely my undoing.

I melted into him, whimpering, and finally let him consume me.

And consume me he did. This wasn't a kiss of love. This wasn't even a kiss of lust unbound. This was a kiss of *claiming*, and it was enough to drown me.

Just tonight, I reminded my subconscious. But I nearly broke the kiss to laugh at my own final attempts of bargaining.

Who was I kidding?

Even the devil liked precious things—and this feeling was the most precious of all. We could have consumed each other for minutes, *hours*, and I still would have wanted to continue with this exact moment forever. We ripped at each other's shirts, hair, and anything we could possibly grab from the other, both trying to consume and escape the other. We were a catastrophic consequence of lust and need unbound, even if it meant claiming the other in the purest form.

Aureo pulled away from me. Both of our chests had the pattern of hummingbird wings— breathless and aching, yet craving more flight. My head ached from the pressure of his hands, the feeling of my hair being pulled so much, and the lingering buzz of alcohol. And even still, I didn't want to stop. I wanted more.

This was the pain I craved. The correction, even if brutal, the urge for more.

"Why did you stop?" I asked, gasping for air. Between this damn noose around my neck and his abuse, my chest was practically heaving.

He squinted at me, panting. "For oxygen?"

"Shut up." I slapped at his chest. "Why didn't you finish?" I asked again, moving my hand back to his dick, still slick with my spit. He groaned lightly as I wrapped my fist around him, though the both of us frowned once he moved my hand off his length. A deflated sense of rejection started to fill me. I thought he wanted this.

"The first time I cum with you, I am going to be inside of you. End of discussion."

Never mind.

I don't think I had ever nodded my head so fast.

Who knew this man, the man I have avoided for years, was such a dirty talker?

And who knew I was so desperate? It was border-line sad.

"You are wearing way too much clothing," he breathed against me. His breath was scorching against my own, the mix of mint and whiskey attacking my senses. I was desperate to admit how much I wanted his mouth on mine again. I wanted my whiskey tongue to match with his again.

"What are you going to do about it?" I pushed.

He chuckled again before pushing me backwards, all the way until I landed on the couch. He practically crawled on top of me, though one of his hands slid down to the zipper of my skirt swiftly undoing it. With a few short tugs, and especially a few curses as he pulled my boots off with a loud thud, I was in nothing but the previously tucked in top and panties.

I couldn't help it as my legs closed together, squeezing again. In the past, I had never been ashamed of my liking for sex. But it felt different with Aureo. I knew my panties probably had a wet spot from how needy I was. I was nearly proved right when Aureo's molten gaze moved down my body, almost lighting an icy fire in its wake, until he stopped at the bright, crimson lace and groaned.

He kneeled before me, now resting his figure on the bar's floor, and traced his fingers over the silky material, putting the slightest pressure against my clit. Fiery shivers erupted over my body from his touch and my hips jerked on their own accord.

I needed *this.*

I needed him.

"I have a few ideas," he rasped, catching my gaze just enough to wink, before he began peeling the satin material away from my flesh, eyes never straying from mine.

SIX

AUREO

I had never wanted to consume someone more than I wanted to consume Phoebe Evans.

And while I wasn't a religious man, I was ready to grovel in front of God himself for allowing me the chance to prove to Phoebe how she was the one I would truly worship.

Especially when she was in nothing but her panties and shirt. Even if she was almost half my age.

I was tired of holding back anymore.

Fucking hell, any man would have groveled at

what I stared down at. The thought alone made me want to roar like a beast, staring down at his prey. I wasn't going to be a hypocrite and ever judge Phoebe for having sex with other men, even if I was one jealous son of a bitch. I had been having sex since I was seventeen—I had no place to judge her for anything.

But to see her breathless, tits pressed against that slim top, with drool and smeared lipstick covering her face. To see bruise marks already forming along her pale skin and yet witness how her need for more persisted. I knew no one but me would ever see this sight again.

Even if it meant I had to fight her until the end of it all.

Even if it meant I had to prove to her how I was different.

Even if it meant I had to end them.

I would be a broken record for the rest of my existence, even if it meant I was the broken record that needed to leave scars against her pretty skin.

Fuck, even that sounded enticing.

She stared down at me from my position on the floor as a mixture of lust, frustration, and maybe even acceptance swirled through the absinthe of her eyes. She was a mixed drink of all emotions, and from the wet spot on her panties moments before, I knew that I was sure to have my fill of everything and more soon.

Especially as she kept holding her legs together like she was desperate for something.

Anything.

My chest nearly vibrated by how wet I found her, though I never broke eye contact, even as her breath hitched when I began to spread her legs. Her throat bobbed as she gulped down a mouthful of air, her fingers twitching at her sides. My fingers traced the lips of her cleanly shaved skin. My mouth watered when I finally broke our staring contest to spread the lips of her pussy, only to reveal a bead of arousal clinging to her clit.

Fucking hell. I was a dead man.

"Is this all for me, little girl? Is this how naughty girls react when they're abused and used, or is that just you?" I asked as I leaned down and blew a breath against her clit. The softest of moans escaped her mouth as she tipped her head back from the sensation.

"You're so mean."

"Yes. And you didn't answer my question."

"Probably because you know the damn answer," she snapped. God help me, I nearly wanted to laugh. She was feisty when she didn't get her way.

Too *fuckin'* bad.

I cocked an eyebrow at her and slapped her clit with the palm of my hand lightly. She could have an attitude with me all she wanted, but none of it would go unnoticed. I didn't care if I had to bruise her ass with a paddle or edge her for hours on end—my girl would learn how to show respect if she truly wanted what she desperately craved.

"I'm waiting, Phoebe."

"Yeah, so am I. Are you just going to look at me from your knees all night? What's next, *little boy*? A ring? I always knew you fell fast."

Well, fuck. She wasn't wrong. My cock jumped at the thought, and I was exceedingly grateful that she couldn't see the effect she had on me from her position on the couch. Because the truthful answer was that I would love to kneel before her and worship her all night long one day. I would love to place the biggest ring on her finger one day.

Not tonight, though.

I slapped her clit again, harder. Her face turned bright red as her entire body jolted from the impact. "Little girl, we can do this all night. You can either answer my question or we can bruise this little pussy until you're on the edge. But believe me when I say that I will hold you back from that cliff for eternity if you choose the second option. Over and over again. I could make these pussy lips puffy and ruined, your legs shaking, all while you sob into the leather of this couch."

"You wouldn't," she practically seethed.

I grinned, chuckling when she yelped as two smacks hit her perfect cunt, both in perfect, hard symmetry. Her thighs trembled from the impact, and I hummed my joy and pleasure into her skin as she lifted her right leg and curled it around my shoulder. Her back nearly bowed from the leather beneath her.

She was an absolute vision.

And she liked it when her cunt was abused.

I blew a breath against her clit again. Her pussy practically wept for my touch and I couldn't wait to make her weep for it, too. Once her back was plastered to the couch again, chest heaving and breaths hollow, I tested my theory.

One, two, three, four, five smacks. With each hit, she cried out and I watched as her eyes nearly rolled into the back of her head. Moans and pants filled the space between us and I knew that my cock had never been harder in all of my life. If I looked down, I knew that beads of precum would have been covering my length.

And I truly couldn't help myself from the sinister act of leaning down and drawing her clit into my mouth, biting softly. I wanted nothing more than to flatten my tongue against every outline and crevice of her pelvic area—fuck, of her entire existence—but I somehow maintained some semblance of control, for this one moment. Phoebe's hands nearly shot into my hair as her hips bucked into my mouth. Moans and pants chased in the wake of their movement. Her clit practically throbbed in my mouth and the sensation alone had me grinding my cock into the couch for any semblance of relief, let alone the taste that teased me before I pulled away.

Instantly, I was met with a whine as she fisted my cropped hair. "No," she begged. "Please don't stop. I want this."

Using my pointer and middle fingers, I rubbed her clit in slow circles, gathering the non-stop building of wetness. I kept eye contact with her as my fingers traveled lower, just dipping in her pussy lightly. She tilted her head back again, gasping just from the pads of two fingers.

Fuck, I couldn't wait to fill this girl with my cock.

She begged again. "Please, Aureo. I'll do anything."

"Oh? Anything?" I mocked.

Looking back down at me, she nodded frantically. Deciding to play with her even more—to see how far she would truly go to please me at this point—my slick fingers left her pussy as I traveled down even lower. I watched as her eyes widened when I spread her left leg even farther, pointing it towards the opposite direction, until her toes were pointed like a ballerina on the concrete floor. If I spread her just four inches more, I would have been forcing her to do a near-split, given the way the tendons and muscles clenched tightly.

My gaze moved away from her eyes, down the length of her body, and came to a stop at her entire bottom region.

She was well and truly *dripping*.

Finally, the fingers belonging to my left hand teased at the entrance to her ass. I watched as the panting, forced breath in her chest was completely suspended. A rough chuckle left me as I massaged the rim of her ass with those same wet, cum-coated fingers. "I seem to remember someone saying that I couldn't tell the difference between an asshole and a clit, little one. A wretched, misbehaved little slut. Do you recall anything of that nature?"

"N-no," she stuttered. I looked back into her bright red face and grinned wickedly.

"No? Oh, I remember it very clearly. I believe she told me that I wouldn't even know how to make a girl come if I tried. What mean words for such a pretty little mouth."

Her chest never stopped its rapid rate of rising and falling. "Maybe you deserved it at the time?"

I narrowed my eyes at her, even as my lips twisted into a sinister, heated smirk. Her mouth formed into the perfect 'o' shape as I pushed the pad of my finger into the tight, hot rim of her ass. I drew it out again, keeping my eyes on her. She leaned forward slightly, her weight resting on her elbows, watching as spit and cum dripped down her pussy, landing on my finger. Her stomach heaved as I pushed that finger back into her hole with the added lubricant.

Her right leg tightened even further against my shoulder as I continued my ministrations, ignoring her pussy entirely. She begged again. "Please, Aureo."

"Please, *what*? Haven't you been a brat tonight? Why should I give a little girl like you anything you crave?" I hissed, spitting at her ass another time. "You have denied me everything tonight. You have denied me for fucking *years*. Why should I give you anything you beg for?"

She hiccupped as she moaned, and I looked up to see tears lining her eyes. I didn't stop my ministrations, though. People cried for lots of reason; I trusted that she would have told me if I was hurting her. By the way her thigh continued to tremble against my shoulder, I had the feeling it was the complete opposite of pain.

She continued. "I'm sorry, okay? I was being a bitch on purpose. You know that. You're right. I'm sorry. Just, *please*."

"Oh, little girl, I know you were being a bitch. I'm asking you to tell me *why*. Plus, it seems like I don't know what a clit is, remember? Poor, poor little girl. Guess you won't be getting anything tonight," I grunted, fucking her with my fingers even harder. Her ass gripped my fingers in a vice and my hips rotated forward when I thought about stuffing my dick in this tight, hot, little hole one day. "I'm a slow learner."

She shuddered against me and I could tell she was getting close just from me playing with her ass alone. Her body was growing as taut as a bow-string. She only needed something final to throw her off the edge of that cliff.

"Aureo," she whined again.

"I swear to God, Phoebe. If you don't tell me, I will leave you just like this. You have five seconds to tell me before I walk out the door and I will never look at this precious piece of ass again. Better yet, I will put duct tape on this pussy so every time you look at another man, you'll remember pulling it off like a wrathful little whore."

Five. The moans and whines continued.

Four. I let go of her left leg, but she instantly wraps

it around my other shoulder, locking both of her legs around my head. The new position instantly makes her tighter against my fingers and I groaned from how forcefully I began to shove my fingers into her. It had to be painful at this point.

Three. The tendons and veins in my forearms bulged from the exertion of pounding into her. Her moans elevated to an ever-higher octave and I swore I could have come all over that damn couch in just that moment.

Two.

"Phoebe," I nearly shouted at her. I meant what I said, but I really didn't want to walk away without her cum all over my hand.

"I want you to hurt me! I want you to abuse me. Bruise me, smack me, wreck me. I wanted you to fuck me as hard as you possibly can and teach me how to be good for you. I want you to fucking keep me if you can do it," she screamed, the sound filled with tortured sobs. "Please, Aureo. I'm begging you. Please let me finish. I want to do it so bad. Please!"

Fucking *finally*.

Would you look at that? I'm a teenage boy who found out what the clitoris was.

"Since you learned how to ask nicely, baby," I groaned into her, finally diving down into her pussy, licking all the way from her taint to her clit. Her hands immediately went to my hair once more as my stubble rubbed against her swollen flesh. My tongue circled her bud before I gave it all of my attention, sucking and nibbling.

"Oh, oh, oh fuck," she moaned against me, bucking her hips into my face wildly, taking whatever she needed. For the first time tonight, I let her do whatever she wished. I was a starved man for this girl and I needed it just as badly as she did, even if I pretended like I didn't. Within minutes, her legs were shaking wildly. "I'm gonna come, Aureo. Fuck, I'm gonna come."

I released her clit to pound into her ass even harder, slipping in a second finger. "Come for me, little girl. Give it to me. Cream all over me. Let's see how tight this ass can get, yeah?" I said, struggling to even get the words out as my own hips gyrate into the couch. I could feel my own orgasm crashing through me, just from getting her off, and it took every morsel of my soul to hold off from denying my cock and impregnating the goddamn couch.

Phoebe clenched even tighter against my fingers as she screamed out my name. Her back nearly bowed entirely off of the couch, with her weight being supported solely from her grip on my shoulders and her own head digging into the rough texture of the red material beneath us.

"Oh my God," she cried out, eyes squeezed shut. I dove my head back down to drink everything she could possibly give me. Her hips bucked into my mouth in overstimulation, but it didn't stop me. Seconds, hours, days, or an eternity later—any amount of time wouldn't have been enough—she gradually rode out every wave of her orgasm until she collapsed in a heap of exhaustion. Sweat lined her thighs, stomach, neck, and every crevice of skin available to the eyes.

What a little devil.

Knowing that the abuse she had endured would have made her ultra-sensitive for the time being, I transitioned all harsh movements into gentle glides of my tongue and fingers, drawing out her orgasm as much as possible while cleaning all of the juices and cream that I possibly could. Her moans and whimpers slowly faded into soft sighs, and when I looked up into her face, I was met with a sleepy, gentle smile. She winced slightly as I moved her hips to the end of the couch before gently removing my fingers from her rear.

I see. So, orgasms calmed the brat.

I was going to be okay with that.

"Sorry, baby girl," I whispered halfheartedly.

"Shut up," she mumbled with a smile. Her hair

may have well matched a lion's mane and it was an erotic sight itself—even without the nearly naked woman attached. There would always be something so stunning about a messy woman, and it was a damned shame they tried to hide it from us.

Standing, I groaned as my body stretched from the cramped position I was previously in. Yet, still achingly hard, I fisted my cock with my right hand, moaning loud and clear. Looking down, I found the tip nearly purple with soul-crushing need.

Grinding into the couch certainly did not relieve the need whatsoever.

Phoebe perked up automatically, twisting to remove her shirt. I groaned as her tits practically bounced from the movement.

Thank fuck she wanted this as much as I did.

She giggled, though it ended in a moan when I leaned forward and pinched one of her nipples. I never stopped the ministrations on my own body—even as precum started building at a rapid pace and I could feel my core clenching. "Round two?"

She spread her thighs again, dipping her fingers back in between her wet, pretty lips. "If these are the orgasms I get, I am totally going to keep you."

My heart soared. "Is that a promise?"

She swirled a piece of her sex-crazed hair around

her finger, biting her lip. "I don't know. You could be horrible in bed. Don't you know the saying?" I watched as she started rubbing her clit achingly slow, groaning softly. The insides of her thighs were creamy and slick.

"What saying?" I growled out.

A giggle met me. "You need to ride the horse and make sure it's right for you before you buy it and ride it forever."

This.

Fucking.

Girl.

"Get on your fucking hands and knees, little girl."

SEVEN

PHOEBE

My knees ached against the floor as my back bowed slightly under Aureo's touch as he skidded his calloused fingers up and down my back slowly. The simple, mindless touch felt so good, even in my desperate state of absolute need for more. I practically felt my brain turning into a puddle from the soft yet demanding attention.

"What should I do with you, sweet girl?"

"Anything," I quickly responded. "Absolutely

anything. I'm yours for the night. I want you to do whatever you want to me."

"Well, I think the things I want to do to you go far past the limitation of one night." A shiver raked itself down my spine at the words. They held a promise, and I didn't know if I should be afraid or welcomed to the idea.

Secretly, I had always wanted to be owned. All of my life, even when I was a little girl, I knew I was protected and loved by dozens of men. But that never took away the loneliness I felt. That loneliness grew into an ache for ownership as I grew into adulthood. I had always been confused about it, though. It wasn't like I wanted a collar and a leash around my throat.

Or I did and I was just really fucking tired of lying to myself.

But, the better question was, did I want Aureo to be the one who held that title? The title of owning me?

How could I possibly want that from only one night?

"You're thinking very loud. Your body is tense," Aureo said, breaking my rapidly growing thoughts. "What is it?"

A hysterical laugh fell out of me. "There is something wrong with me."

His fingers on my back halted mid trek, pushing

down on the middle of my back until I was forced into an arching position. "And why do you say that?"

"Because it's true," I snapped. My quickly sated state evaporated, filling with irritation instead. I wasn't used to someone wanting inside my head and I still didn't know how to feel about him. This could only be one night. I wasn't going to let someone into my head after a one night stand. That was how attachment issues become stalker-level.

A deep sigh flitted through Aureo. His fingers continued this ministrations, slowly crawling up my back until they reached my hair. Suddenly, he grabbed the base of my skull, fisting my long, black hair into a knot around his fist and pulled roughly. "And here I thought I could fuck the brat out of you. Is this how you're going to be all night?" I met him in silence. My brain was unbelievably overstimulated from the amount of thoughts racing through me and I didn't know if I was going to weep, beg, or spontaneously combust.

He continued, tsking under his breath. "Phoebe, Phoebe, Phoebe. If I had known you liked avoiding questions so much, I would have kept gagging you."

"Maybe you should have."

"Oh, really? Is that what you want?"

I wish he would get the fucking hint. I didn't know what I wanted. I wanted someone to decide that for me, for fucks sake. I wanted to not make a single decision at all.

Instead, I said, "Yes."

Before I could blink, Aureo's hold on my hair disappeared, forcing my neck to go slack. I nearly whimpered from the loss of contact and strain I didn't know I was even enjoying. Moments later, his hand tilted my face up, forcing my eyes to land on his molten gaze. The brown in his gaze felt midnight black, though I knew for a fact that when he was smiling or near sunlight, they would turn into the finest of honey.

Too captivated in his gaze, I hardly noticed my bunched up, wet panties in his hand until the sound of them ripping filled the heated air.

Anger hit me again. "What the fuck? I liked those!" I whined.

"Oh, drop the fucking prideful princess act for a fucking minute. I'll buy you a new pair."

Before I could come back with a matching retort, the lacy material was shoved in my mouth, effectively silencing anything I could have ever said. A flitting sense of shame filled me as the taste of my own arousal hit my tongue. Quickly, he tied my own panties around my head, knotting them at the back of my skull until my mouth was open and cheeks were spread roughly. He finished tying the knot and moments after, a harsh smack landed on my ass, forcing a muffled whine out of me. I *loved* it.

"Oh, would you look at you now. Fuck, you look like such a good girl when you're this vulnerable for me. On your hands and knees, back arched, gagged and silent like the doll you should be. Should I take a picture for you to see?"

I shook my head. Absolutely not. I did not need to see how pitiful I looked like this, at the mercy of another man's touch and attention. I already felt the drool seeping down my chin from the odd position of my mouth. The last thing I needed was to *see* it.

He laughed mockingly. "Oh, you don't have a choice. I can do whatever the fuck I want to you while you're like this. Do you understand me?"

I looked up at him, eyes filling with tears. I didn't even know why I was crying at this point. Rather than any look of pity or attraction in his gaze, I was met with a devilish smirk instead. Looking around, he reached over me. Thinking he was going to smack my ass again, I wiggled it towards him, only to be met with yet another mocking laugh.

"So, so eager. Such an eager little girl," he whispered, humor filling his tone into a mocking rather than supportive setting. I looked back at him, nearly drooling from the sight of his filled frame and bobbing cock, only to stop short when I noticed the cell phone in his hand.

Fuck.

Double fuck.

What had I gotten myself into?

The sound of a camera shutter mixed with my heaving puffs of air. Aureo bit his lip as he stared down at his phone. I nearly came undone when he wrapped a hand around his length, stroking slowly to the picture he just took of me.

As much as I wanted to deny it, my legs clenched together from watching him. I was right there, *right there* for his complete and utter taking, and yet he still continued to touch himself to the picture of me rather than using me for his needs instead.

It was absolutely humiliating. I felt my cheeks grow even warmer than they already were. But I couldn't stop the ache in between my legs growing by the second.

"You're an absolute fucking goddess, even when I've forced you to be my own personal slave." Pleasure raked through me at his praise. He looked back at me, smiling roughly before he turned his phone in my direction. Immediately, my eyes landed on the photo of me and my own gasps turned into one of pleasure.

I looked like a fucking mess. My hair was crazed, wildly sticking up in multiple directions. My body was coated in a sheen of sweat, even noticeable to the camera. Drool dripped its way down my chin, going as far as to make my nipples look wet. You could even see the faint outline of a handprint on my ass from the angle of the picture.

"Beautiful, isn't it?" Aureo said, pride filling his tone. "I think I'll have the framed and put on my fucking desk."

Goddamn me to hell. But instead of irritation or anger from the words, a sense of longing filled me instead. Throwing his phone down on the couch, Aureo leveled me with a dark gaze. The look alone nearly gave me cottonmouth and I really didn't think it was because of the panties. "You're going to answer some questions for me. No bratty tones—not like you can speak anyway —and no ignoring me. Do you understand?"

For the smallest of seconds, a war raged in my brain. I didn't know if I should answer him.

But *fuck*. I was tired of fighting him, and more

importantly, I was tired of fighting what I wanted. So, I took a leap of faith instead. I nodded my head.

A genuine smile came over him. It melted me entirely. "Good girl. Now, do you like feeling like this?"

Yes. I nodded my head.

"Do you like being a little whore for me?"

One thousand times, *yes.* He received the same response.

"Hmmm, good girl. Now, here is the important question," he started. He walked around me, leaving my line of vision, but I felt his gaze crawling down my entire body. His rough hands landed on my ass again, filling the air with a smacking noise. I bit down on my panties as I moaned around them. It burned like hell. "Do you want to see me again after tonight? Do you want this? Everything this entails?"

Hesitation coursed through me. I felt my body stiffen from his question.

This was too fast. I knew it was too fast.

But I felt euphoric. And I wanted to feel this way forever.

I just hoped it wouldn't be a mistake.

I nodded my head.

"Thank *fuck*," he growled back. Moments later, I

finally felt the tip of his cock tease the entrance of my pussy. "Last question. Do you want me to fuck you?"

I barely managed a single, full head nod before he speared through me roughly, his entire length entering me in one thrust, forcing a scream to flit through my throat.

EIGHT

AUREO

I had died. I had died and I had gone to heaven. That had to be the case, right? Because fuck, there was no way on Earth I was anywhere close to hell if this is how good it felt.

Phoebe moaned around me as I filled her aching pussy. My dick was so slick with her cum that it coated my length entirely. I swore I started seeing stars when she clenched on my length.

"Fuuucckkkk," I moaned, grabbing her hips roughly. I only hoped that I would leave bruise marks

on her flesh. I had fantasized and jerked off to this girl more times than I could count on both hands. I had done the absolutely crazy, insane notion of picturing her while I fucked other girls.

It didn't matter. None of it had felt this good. I practically felt a lightning bolt zap down my spine.

I pushed her down by her neck, forcing her head all the way down onto the dirty bar floor. Realistically, I knew she was probably pressing her cheek into dirt, spilled alcohol, and whatever mysterious substances fell onto bar floors, but I couldn't give a single flying fuck. I needed this. I needed her.

Most of all, I needed her to know who she belonged to now. Even if that meant I needed to shove her face into a dirty floor.

Her filthy, muffled moans dragged into the air as I started moving, shifting my hips to get as deep as I possibly could. I thrusted into her hard, wrapping my fist around her onyx strands again, forcing her into the floor even more as I mounted her sweet body. Her entire body shook with the thrust and it was all the motivation I needed to properly ruin her over and over again. I pumped into her over and over again, moans and slick sounds filling around us. My teeth sawed into my bottom lip as pleasure racked throughout my core.

"Do you like that, you filthy slut? Is this what you

needed? Did you need to be filled to take that little ache away?" A garbled moan met me in agreement. A dark chuckle left me as I relinquished the grip on her neck, tugging the panties out of her mouth.

There would be other nights that I would edge and tease Phoebe with a proper ball gag for hours. Tonight? I wanted to hear her beg.

I was only rewarded for doing so. "Fuck," she moaned. "Fuck, yes. Yes, Aureo. Please don't stop. Please don't stop. It feels so fucking good. You feel so good."

"Yeah? Tell me what you like. Tell me what you want, dirty girl."

"You," Phoebe sobbed, clawing her wine colored nails—the color of her now ruined lipstick—into the ground as if she were trying to break into the building's flooring itself. "I want you to use me, fuck me, and hurt me however you please."

I groaned loudly as I thought about all the things I wanted to do to this girl. She was so fucking lucky we were on her daddy's bar floor instead of my bed. In the proper setting, I would belt her until her ass was covered in lines and welts—maybe even blood if she craved it.

I settled on slapping her ass as I thrusted into her repeatedly, leaving fat, red hand print marks all over her flesh. Her skin was fiery red as I continued to abuse her. I couldn't tell if the sounds coming out of her mouth were moans or sobs, but I relished in it, nonetheless.

"This ass is mine, Phoebe. Do you understand me?" I growled. She mewled in response as her pussy fluttered along my length. She was close. "Do you *fucking* understand me?"

"Yes!" she shouted.

"Yes, what? What do you understand?"

"Please, Aureo. I want to come so fucking bad. Please don't make me say it." Hearing her words, I stopped, hips pressed fully against hers. I wasn't big enough to hurt her but I pressed my weight into her all the same, forcing myself and my swollen tip as deep as it could go. Immediately, she whined and begged, pushing herself back onto me to try and fuck herself.

I smirked, dragging my hands away from her throat and underneath her. I pinched her nipples in between my fingers and twisted before making my way to her clit and rubbing softly. The pads of my fingers just barely brushed against my own length and it was a miracle I didn't blow into her. Her breath hitched and her body grew tense as I played with her.

"You're going to tell me what I want to fucking

hear or you're not going to come," I whispered roughly.

"No," Phoebe whined. "No, please. Please let me come."

"Tell me what I want to hear, little girl." I rubbed at her bud faster, forcing her legs to shake. I wasn't going to force her to spell it out for me this time. I wasn't going to yell at her. I was simply going to make her brainless.

"Fuck," she panted. "I'm close, baby. Yes! Don't stop."

I laughed, slowing down. "I'll do whatever I want. You seem to forget who is in charge a lot."

"Why do you hate me?" she whined, bucking back into me again.

"Hate you? Oh, baby girl. Why can't you see it? I'm fucking *obsessed* with you."

Her entire body shuddered at the sentiment as the word vomit followed. "Fine! Fine, I'll fucking say it, you asshole. I'm yours. I'll be yours. My ass is yours to do whatever you want with. Just, please, let me come. I'll be good. Please, Aureo."

I thank whatever God I can every day that she wasn't able to see the smile that lit up my face from her words. My left hand squeezed her thigh as hard as I possibly could as I started fucking her again, thrusting insistently while rubbing her clit at the same time. Her head snapped back as pleasure coursed through her, showing itself in her moans all the way to her legs trying to spread and shift all at the same time. I placed my left hand on her head, forcing her down again, and tugged the belt to restrict her airflow more. I didn't want her to have any control at that moment. I would give this girl the world one day, but in that moment, she was just a hole for my pleasure.

And fuck, she was fucking gorgeous when she was desperate.

"C'mon, baby," I growled, rubbing her clit in furious circles. "Come for me. Come all over my cock. I got you."

"Fuck, fuck! Fuck, yes!" she screamed with her panting mixing in to her chorus. Her orgasm wracked throughout her body wildly, forcing her eyes shut as she ground her cheek into the cold floor. Her mouth popped open, forcing me to see stars the moment her tongue started peeking out like she was a cam girl in a teenage boy's favorite film. Groaning along with her, I warned her, "I'm going to come. I'm going to blow for you, little girl. Where do you want it?"

"In me," she nearly pleaded. "Come in me baby!"

Fist still in her hair, pinning her fragile body, my back bowed as an orgasm climbed its way through me.

Heat coursed through my entire body like heroin did from an addict's favorite needle. I ground my teeth together as it hit, pumping my hips into her even harder, filling her with as much cum as she could possibly take.

Whimpers left her as I pulled out, only to spread her with my fingers, watching as the cum seeped out of her and started dripping onto the floor.

So many thoughts wire themselves through my skull.

She was gorgeous when she leaked what I gave her.

She was mine.

And, importantly, I was most definitely going to clean that couch, floor, and whatever else we had touched before her father paid his dear strip club a visit.

Hell, I may need to just build him a new club now.

That girl was mine.

Our story had just begun.

EPILOGUE

PHOEBE

Days passed.

I felt like an absolute idiot for doing it, but I hardly left my house in fear of seeing Aureo, even to go down the street to the local convenience store.

I had my tubs of ice cream *delivered*.

That's desperation.

The self-isolation was on a new level, and I knew Echo or my dad were going to behead me if I didn't speak to them soon, but it was worth it for the time being.

I still didn't know what to think or feel after the night Aureo and I shared at the Crow Cavern. Wallowing in self-induced pity was better than nothing.

I had spent the past week in nothing but a pair of leggings and a sweatshirt I had owned since I was in high school, burying myself in comfort TV shows like *Pretty Little Liars*, and consuming far too much ice cream.

In some circumstances, this would be considered self-care, but I knew myself more than that. I knew I was avoiding the reality of my situation.

I was pathetic.

Being with Aureo was the best sex of my life.

Hell, it was the best birthday of my life.

Yet, when I woke up the next morning still wrapped up in his arms on my dad's couch, I still felt that ownership in a way that made my knees weak and my heart palpitate wildly. And I didn't know if I was even allowed to feel that way.

We had agreed on one thing. Just for that night.

Then life would go back to normal.

Somehow, my wildest dreams and fantasies had come true all in the matter of a single night, and I ended up wanting to take them back because I wasn't allowed to feel the happiness I craved the morning after again. Especially because I was the one who told him to fuck off most of the time.

It was a night with a man who was twenty years my senior. And it was with a man who had known me since I was a fragile teenager who begged for attention every day of my life. Why did I want him more than ever now?

What kind of person did that make me? What kind of person did that make us, if there even *was* an us? Sure, Aureo and I had said some heated things in the moment, but did that make it a reality? Everyone loved dirty talk.

I didn't even know what being owned felt like. I didn't even know what genuine romantic love felt like.

I had never allowed anyone close enough.

And there I was, wishing Aureo would do it anyway.

I sighed, scrubbing my forehead in frustration.

Everything was so confusing. I should have just stayed celibate. I was far past the limitation of becoming a nun, but I could have celebrated my birthday with a tattoo and a sprinkle of holy water, right?

A deep huff left me next as I stared at my TV

screen. Of course, it was a scene where one of the girls began kissing their teacher, highlighting all the forbidden nature that surrounded me and my current predicament.

Even with those facts, I didn't *really* care. It wasn't like we did anything wrong. We were both more than legal, age-gap relationships were perfectly normalized in our day and age, and kink is only an up-hill conversation.

There was absolutely nothing wrong with what we did.

There was nothing wrong with finding pleasure in someone you never knew you would.

I had to shake myself out of the pit of depression I had somehow fallen into.

It wasn't like I had been broken up with. I wasn't wishing hatred on all men, holding up a ball of angst against the entire male population.

In reality, I was the one who had disappeared.

But, alas, the ice cream in my freezer sounded far more enticing.

Much, much more enticing than the dozens of texts and calls from Aureo on my phone. Ghosting people may not be recommended, but man, was it better than facing reality.

My shoulders slumped forward as a harsh knock sounded at my door.

Go. Away.

I hated when people showed up unannounced. It was almost worth it to purchase a snarky doormat for anyone who dared disturb me and my pessimistic brain. I'm sure there had to be a small business who sold one that said something along the lines of, *Bibbidi-Bobbidi-Boo, This Door is Not for You*, with a poisoned skull symbol right on top.

Hell, I would've sold them myself if I knew how.

I was almost positive it would have become a best-seller.

Deciding to keep up with my never-ending pessimistic streak, I shouted as loud as possible, "Phoebe isn't here. Please leave a message!"

An answering, pounding knock set my teeth on edge.

"I'm in the middle of watching the most grotesque, CNC, rape-filled porn! Please return at a later date when I am not otherwise preoccupied."

Knock.

Knock.

Knock.

"Fucking hell," I snapped angrily, jolting as whoever's fist nearly punched a hole through my door. I threw the blanket off of me and stomped to the entrance of my apartment, practically moving to the door like an annoyed grandmother who is about to throw a shoe at someone's head. Swinging the door open, I spit, "Listen, buddy. I just want to watch my fuck–"

"Oh, I heard," Aureo said, cutting me off and glowering down at me from his tall frame. "CNC porn, eh? I knew you liked it rough, but I didn't peg you for that one. I can always try it, though. I'm down to try anything once."

My mouth snapped shut as my back was forced ramrod straight, shoulders pinched back.

He wasn't wearing his mask.

Oh, it was a personal visit then. *Fuck.*

And yet, my legs closed together from instant sex flashbacks anyway.

My eyes raked down his form, taking in every piece of him that I possibly could with what was visible. He wore dark jeans over his leather biker boots, though they hugged his thighs more than they had the right to, and wore nothing more than a black t-shirt with his thumbs now tucked in his jean pockets. His shorter-length hair was wild, showcasing how he definitely rode here on his bike, and the snake tattoo I had admired since I was a teenage girl showed itself on his bicep from the way he was holding his arms.

I practically had to stop myself from drooling.

Not happening.

"You know, you could have punched a damn hole in my door with how hard you were pounding on it," I glowered, turning around to look at my front door and make sure there actually wasn't a hole waiting for me.

There wasn't one. Damnit.

I wanted an excuse to kick him for making me an emotional mess.

Turning back to him, I glared with one eyebrow perfectly poised, waiting for him to speak, only to be met with silence.

Perfect.

We were back to the game.

I rolled my eyes and shook my head, already coming to terms with where this was going. "Alright, well this has been fun. It's lovely seeing your face in daylight once again. Have a good one," I said, turning around and going to shut the door.

I nearly had it shut when he spoke again, voice darker than sin. "You've been avoiding me."

I turned back to him slowly, cocking my head ever so slightly. "Were you wanting to chat? Possibly over a set of tea and crumpets?"

"You don't like tea."

I squinted at him, forehead scrunching. "How could you possibly know that?"

He stepped forward and leaned against the doorframe, forcing me farther into my apartment and effectively trapping me from slamming the door in his face again. "You don't like tea. You don't even like coffee, unless it's your fancy as fuck espresso lattes. Your favorite color is purple, but you're also extremely particular over the different shades and you could rant about it for an hour, at least. And your favorite classic book is *Frankenstein* because you have an infatuation with the dark sides of life and death, like a fucking weirdo."

Well, fuck.

I sniffed. "I'll have you know tha–"

He continued, stepping forward once more. Twice. I moved backwards. "I'm not finished. You only like desserts that have cream cheese icing on them. You haven't had a boyfriend since you were nineteen because you're afraid of commitment or something. Your favorite flowers are white jasmine. And you're the farthest thing from a disrespectful brat, but you don't feel like you always get the attention you truly crave which makes you act out like a little bitch sometimes."

Well, now I was properly offended.

And confused as to how he knew that much about me.

No one knew that much about me.

"Okay, stalker, I need you to sto–"

He pushed me lightly into the foyer wall, leaving my door wide open as he towered over me, effectively dismissing any personal space. My hoodie pressed against his midsection and I became painfully aware of my lack of undergarments at that moment. "You're scared of life. You're scared of living. And you're even more scared of taking a chance and falling in love. But the best part of this situation is that I'm tired of waiting for you to open your goddamned eyes. So, you don't have a fucking choice."

My breath stilled in my chest.

I tilted my gaze toward him, brain short-circuiting. I almost didn't know what to say.

There was zero sass left in my defeated tone as I responded, "Are you finished?"

"Two more things," he whispered, tucking a lock of hair behind my ear before leaning down. He forced a shiver through me as his stubble grated against my ear and face. "You want this, or you wouldn't have let me into your apartment without ruining my chance of future children, and you're not watching CNC porn. You're watching another one of your god-awful teenage dramas. CNC porn would be too exciting for you."

Dickweed.

Deciding against my brain's judgment, I fisted his t-shirt as he stood up straight, ensuring he wasn't going anyway. I watched his eyes as he studied mine, and I questioned him more than I ever had. Most of all, I questioned why he wanted a life with me, why he wasn't giving me a choice to fight against him, when I was the one who was terrified of everything and he wasn't.

I said exactly that. "I'm scared."

"I know."

"I don't know what this means. We shared one night. We would be crazy to act off of that."

"I know that, too. I've thought about it all week. But you know just as well as I do that this has been more than a single night. Our silent feuds were just years of foreplay."

Tears lined my eyes at his words and I cursed my hidden emotions. I hoped I could just blame it on PMSing. "Yeah?"

Lamest response of the year.

He chuckled, using his forefinger and thumb on my chin to tip my head up even more. "Baby girl, you haven't left my thoughts for a single minute. I even dreamt about you. Do you know how obsessed a man has to be in order to dream about living life with his girl? We prefer sex and chaos in those things."

A wet laugh escaped me. "I don't know what this means. I hardly know anything about you. You can't just move in right away, you know?"

"I never asked for that. I said you were giving us a chance. We'll go from there."

"My father is going to kill you, you know? He may even try to castrate you with a motorcycle."

"I literally shot a hole in his club's ceiling to fuck you. He's already beating hellfire down my neck. Castration would only be the cherry on top, wouldn't you think? Why not go all the way?" A crooked smile fit his face and my breath hitched as I stared at him, dropping all defenses.

I snorted. How romantic.

I was right, though, I noticed as I stared up at him.

His eyes turned into liquid honey when he was happy.

A hysterical laugh flitted out of me then. "So, this is what you want? You want a brat with a severe attitude problem? You want a girl who's gonna fight you in her fear of everything? A girl who acts out until you hurt and abuse her? Weird choice."

"Fuck yes, I do," he responded in complete seriousness. "And if it makes me weird, then we'll be a little screwed up together."

I shook my head, even as I leaned into him more. "You're crazy. You could be my dad."

He took my hand in his, holding it tightly before he leaned down once more. "Maybe a little bit," he whispered before he pressed his mouth to mine. I stood on my tiptoes and melted into him. He kissed me passionately, *wildly*, and it was magical.

It was us.

He lifted his head away from mine and whispered with a dark smile, "Don't ever compare me to your dad again, though."

I giggled at his tone.

"Oh? Why don't you like that, *Daddy*? Maybe I could behave."

His eyes dilated from the word and I made a mental note to myself...

Oh, this will be fun.

Shaking my head, I yanked his head back down to mine, desperate to kiss him again.

I didn't know why I trusted him.

I didn't know why I trusted my gut for a happy future at that moment.

I didn't even know why I let him shut the door to my apartment and carry me to my couch, where he laughed and mocked me as he found the teenage angst awaiting me on my living room TV, only to keep kissing me.

And I definitely didn't know why I automatically agreed with him when he told me that I belonged to him.

But it was us. And I liked the idea of us more than anything.

Even if it took some blind trust.

ACKNOWLEDGMENTS

In complete honestly, I don't even know where to start in this section, which is the most ironic thing of all. Isn't it funny how us writers can write full blown love stories, complete with spice and happily-ever-afters, and yet, we pause when we need to reflect on our real life? I do, anyway. All the same, there are so many people I need to thank and mention throughout this section.

First and foremost, I want to thank everyone who pushed me to publish this, even when the self-doubt crept in so severely that I wondered if I could do it at all. This list is long, but ranges from all the names of Katie, Eli, Jillian, Charly, Angie, Tilly, Havoc W., and more. All of you, in some variation, led me to finally get the courage to publish this debut, and it's been one of the scariest things of my life. I love you all, in all of our weird ways. I consider you all friends. That said, you're not allowed to leave me now... because I have issues.

To fellow authors in the book community (not mentioned above) including but not limited to Cyn, Sage, Taylor, Bethanie, London, Dana, Suzi, Cass, and more—thank you for not only helping me with my innocent questions, but for supporting me too. It genuinely means a lot. I don't know how I would have made it this far without all of you.

To my parents, who always said, "I knew you'd do it one day." I don't necessarily think this is the direction you thought I'd take... but, hey... I made it, didn't I? For the love of God, don't read this though. I'm already mortified putting you in here.

To my sisters, who... honestly, don't even know what a dust jacket is, but still support me all the same. I'm glad we've gotten closer in the recent years.

To my nieces, nephew, and dog, who kept me alive at really dark times in my life, even if they didn't know it. Your innocence gives me fresh air.

To English Proper Editing Services, thank you so much for taking me last minute, with the very manic decision of me deciding to press publish. Your feedback still makes me giggle.

To Havoc Archives (aka, father), insert a, "Forgive me father, for I have sinned," moment here. I still appreciate you. And you deserve to be mentioned in another book. I know you'll pout.

To AnnaRoseReading, did you know that you were one of the first people I even told about this book, all the way when we met so long ago? Oh, how so much has happened since then. Thank you for being just as excited for me now as you were then.

And lastly, to T, who always believed I could do this, even when I didn't. You say things like, "I didn't do anything to help you get here," but I firmly disagree. You've dealt with many spirals, many tears, many manic moments, and more. You've given me writing "assignments" to break my slumps, realistic advice from someone not in the romance community, and just... love. You've turned my emo, black heart to a shade of yellow just for you, and you deserve to be in here, even if you grunt like a caveman. Own it, you stubborn wizard. You're lucky this is all I'm putting. PS: Thanks for the name suggestion.

ABOUT THE AUTHOR

C. S. Silverne is a twenty-something year old author who spends a lot of her time hiding behind a computer as the true introvert she is—between writing words, designing pretty pictures, reading her kindle, or blaring the latest rock music release—it's guaranteed she's trying to ignore the world in some emo fashion.

Even in her dark/forbidden and occasionally taboo writing styles... she takes light of her pseudonym, always finding love in the silver linings of the world. Because, as we all know, sometimes—love chooses us in the strangest, cruelest of ways, and the stories of the forbidden deserved to be told.

https://www.cssilverneauthor.com/